Fanning the Fantasy

New *X Rated* titles from *X Libris*:

The *X Libris* series:

Fanning the Fantasy

Zara Devereux

www.xratedbooks.co.uk

An *X Libris* Book

First published in Great Britain as *Saturnalia*
in 1995 by X Libris
This edition published in 2002

A CIP catalogue record for this book
is available from the British Library.

ISBN 0 7515 3256 8

Typeset by
Derek Doyle & Associates, Liverpool
Printed and bound in Great Britain by
Clays Ltd, St Ives plc

X Libris
An imprint of
Time Warner Books UK
Brettenham House
Lancaster Place
London WC2E 7EN

Chapter One

THE TALL, DARK, voluptuous woman replaced the telephone receiver in its gilded rest and relaxed on the black leather chesterfield. She smiled to herself and took a sip of champagne, thinking about the caller. Another satisfied customer in more ways than one. He couldn't wait to come back.

She thought about her business, a hobby as well as a lucrative source of income. Not only that; every bit of her considerable acting talent was called upon, and she revelled in it. Xanthia Delaney, who had struggled through drama school – and struggle it had been until she found a man who was willing to pay her handsomely to appear in his exclusive type of movies. Some might class them as unworthy, even degrading, but to her they were simply doing what came naturally, doing it well, and in public.

She had come far since those early days. A rich marriage, an even more productive divorce, and here she was in her lovely country house which had proved to be not only a home, but another profit-making venture, too. Enjoying a moment of peace before the influx of further, fee-paying guests she allowed her eyes to dwell on the stately drawing-room in which she lounged. This part of the house was Tudor. It was rich in linen-fold panelling. The ceiling was a riot of plaster swags and paintings of nude goddesses with rosy-tipped breasts and dimpled backsides, frollicking amidst cushiony clouds with horned, hairy satyrs wielding enormous phalluses.

Xanthia's senses stirred as she contemplated these Arcadian scenes. She wriggled against the leather, a coil of pleasure tightening in her womb at the feel of her emerald green silk robe slithering against her skin. It clung to every curve of her body, and she was intensely aware of the material chafing her nipples which sprang instantly erect, hard as stones.

She drew a fold tightly between her thighs, rubbing it over her secret lips, but this did not entertain her for long. She needed something more than masturbation that afternoon. Restless, she rose to her feet and began to prowl the room, lithe and catlike, the compulsive need in her as urgent as that of a pedigree Siamese queen, the randiest of felines when on heat.

Sometimes she missed the heady excitement of the film world – the parties, the galas, the sexual adventures. But here, within her own walls, she had everything to compensate, an unlimited selection of partners, a golden opportunity to perfect her craft, looking on it as an art. The techniques, the sets, the scenery, the costumes, all mysterious adjuncts to the field in which she was an expert.

She crossed the thick-pile Persian patterned carpet, bare feet padding softly, toes curling in appreciation of its plush depths, and made her way out into the hall. Here the icy contrast of the black and white tiles made her shiver pleasurably. This was the secret. To plumb the extremes of sensation. Pain, pleasure, it was all one to her. She made her way up the magnificent staircase with its balustrades comprised of writhing serpents, fingers relishing the smooth texture of the wood, and along to her own apartment which few were privileged to see.

This suite was her private place, her den, her domain, large and extravagantly furnished in brooding Gothic style. The arched windows were swagged in velvet drapes, with heavily fringed pelmets and tiebacks whose tassels were a foot long. Priceless oriental rugs were strewn like islands on the shiny waters of the parquet flooring. Ornate Venetian mirrors reflected the scene over and over. The crystal drops festooning a central chandelier flashed rainbow shards of light from a ceiling that was as intricately fan-vaulted as a church.

Xanthia's red mouth curled in a smile. The simile is apt, she thought, for this is a sacred place, dedicated to Isis, the Egyptian Goddess of Love.

The *fin de siècle* atmosphere was brooding and sensual. She adored the decadent period at the end of the nineteenth century, admiring its authors, composers, architects, interior designers, poets and playwrights, and collecting memorabilia with the avidity of a magpie. She would travel miles to attend an auction sale where Art Nouveau pieces were up for grabs.

Multi-hued tapestry cushions were piled on the couches that stood either side of the towering marble fireplace, and the bed was monumental, fully seven foot wide and a further seven long. It had been made originally for a king's mistress, its bedspread a vast crimson velvet plane embroidered in gold, the tester rearing up, matching curtains falling from a ruched satin *ciel*.

Xanthia contemplated her room with the

deepest satisfaction; it was her lair, an outward expression of her complex personality. Every aspect of it carried a sexual connotation. There were paintings on the walls and framed erotic prints from Italy, India, China, Turkey and Japan, each showing the male and female in a multitude of positions, frozen in time in sensual esctasy. Lewd statuettes lined the overmantel; monsters mating with humans, men with men, women with women, sometimes the couples so intertwined that it was impossible to tell one from the other. Xanthia, regarding them closely, could feel desire knotting in her belly again, her vulva moistening, clitoris stirring like a small, hungry animal.

She reached for the intercom, which was cunningly concealed by the inlaid headboard of the bed. It connected with her office, and she spoke into it. 'Has Mr Hervieu arrived yet? He has an appointment.'

'Yes, Miss Delaney. He's waiting,' replied the disembodied voice of her secretary.

Xanthia could picture her – bespectacled, plain and prim. No one would guess at the seething cauldron of lust that boiled beneath her sensible skirt, but Xanthia knew. She had been there, had satisfied Miss Jean Chigwell's cravings on many occasions, respecting her as one of the most enthusiastic, dedicated and inventive members of her team.

'Tell him to come up.' Xanthia replaced the phone, amusement rippling through her as she thought, I should have said 'give the boy a wash and send him to my tent!'

Jason Hervieu, out-of-work actor. His agent had suggested that he try Delaney Enterprises. Xanthia had received his CV by post, along with a batch of photographs. A beautiful young man –

4

the studio portraits were subtly lit, emphasising the high cheekbones, the finely chiselled lips, the cleft chin, the black curls falling about his neck and shoulders, and those heavy-lidded, slumberous eyes. He smoulders very well indeed, she thought, examining the photos again as she waited, lascivious tongue peeping out to circle her lips. Yes, I think I can use Jason Hervieu.

When he knocked on the bedroom door, she called to enter. He was taller than she had visualised, a magificently built six-footer who obviously spent a lot of time and energy working out. The black tee-shirt he wore emphasised his tan and outlined the well developed shoulders and chest. His jeans were extremely tight, leaving little to the imagination, and Xanthia admired his bulge as he walked towards her, smiling, a hand extended. He moved with the elegance of a trained dancer, light on his feet for so large a man.

'Miss Delaney,' he said, his voice having that resonance brought about by stage work. 'I've been looking forward to meeting you.'

Xanthia experienced an electric thrill as her fingers met his, that strong tanned hand contrasting with her smaller one. She could see him glancing beyond, noticed the slight shock on his face as he spotted the paintings. A quick glance down registered that his bulge had become more pronounced. A promising start. He was so handsome that she had feared for a moment that he might by gay. But no, his reaction to her and his surroundings was undeniably heterosexual.

'Shall we sit?' She led the way to one of the deeply cushioned couches. 'Would you like a drink?'

Jason shook his head. 'No, thank you, Miss Delaney. I want to keep a clear head.'

Do you indeed? She mused. We'll see about that. Knowing his eyes were glued to her, she sashayed over to the built-in fridge, which was craftily disguised as an oak court-cupboard. Ice-cubes tinkled into a glass of orange juice. She, too, wanted no alcohol to deaden the sensations she was experiencing. Jason was the most stimulating thing she had seen for ages.

They discussed his career for a while, though both were keenly aware of the tension building up between them. He'd had a few minor roles in TV productions and had done several commercials. An American musical had fed him for some months, but this had closed and, at the moment, he was 'resting'.

Xanthia knew what he meant. She, too, had suffered those spells between jobs when money became desperately short and one's faith in one's abilities reached an all time low.

'I signed on the dole for a while,' he said, seated stiffly on the settee, long legs resting open in those skin-tight jeans, big, shapely hands dangling between them. He looked like a young Marlon Brando in *A Streetcar Named Desire*.

'Are you working now?' Xanthia permitted her robe to fall open, displaying her legs as she leaned closer to him. Guerlain's pungent and evocative *L'Heure Bleue* perfumed mingled with her own warm scent breathing out from between her breasts.

'As a garage attendant,' he said huskily, unable to keep his eyes from the triangle glimpsed at the apex of her thighs. The weather had to be extremely cold for Xanthia to wear panties, and at the moment England was going through a heatwave.

'What a waste,' she murmured, pressing her shoulder against his momentarily as she shifted position.

The robe opened further, very casually, as if she was unaware. Nothing could have been further from the truth. She could feel herself growing warmer and looser; it was a good feeling. There was so much to teach him. He'd be a novice, she was convinced of it. But there was all the time in the world – a whole, long sunfilled afternoon if, and only if, he proved an apt pupil and she found him pleasing.

'I'm not certain what you'd want me to do here,' he continued, legs crossed now in an unsuccessful attempt to hide his arousal.

Xanthia lay back against the cushions, her hands clasped behind her head, the action of raising her arms thrusting her breasts higher, the robe parting over the deep valley that divided them. She felt her nipples tighten and tingle against the material, felt the liquid heat between her legs begin to flow. The room was filled with dusky light, dust motes circling and dancing in the rays cast by the strong sun. It bounced off stained glass, and flashed on gilt. Xanthia relished these surroundings, such a useful adjunct to seduction.

'I run an unusal establishment,' she murmured, and trailed her fingers lightly over his muscular upper arm, catching a whiff of *Eternity* as she did so. So he had expensive tastes, had he? Better and better, she thought, adding aloud, 'My staff need to be able to act. I'll explain about this later, if I decide to take you on.'

He was alert now, staring at her, fascinated. 'You want me to give an audition?' he asked unsteadily. 'Recite something from a play? I've brought along a video of the commercials I've been in. Will that do?'

'Don't worry. I'll look at it in a while. I've no doubt you're competent.' Her hand followed the

7

curve of his bronzed forearm, the skin lightly furred, not shaven as that of many weight-training fanatics. He pumped iron to keep his body in shape, not as an end in itself.

'They tell me I'm OK.' More than anything he wanted to impress this extraordinarily lovely woman who was looking at him with those almond-shaped green eyes, hedged by thick black lashes.

'Of course you are, Jason. But we need to go a little further. This is a specialised job. It will be necessary for you to wear period costume from time to time. I'm sure you'll look magnificent.'

Her pulse was thudding, and she permitted her wandering hand to stroke his denim-clad thigh. Oh, she'd enjoy seducing this one, teaching him how to pleasure her and master the refined sensual delights she desired. Almost idly, she ran a pointed, gold-varnished fingernail down the zipper of his jeans, testing the weight and size of him through the material. He was hard, bulging and massive, his erection pointing upwards, against the restriction, rising, rising, almost to his waist.

He drew in a sharp breath, and her mouth moistened with a sudden rush of saliva, matching the wetness of those twin lips enfolding her swollen clitoris which was demanding immediate attention. Slowly, she continued to run her nail along his zipper. Even though schooling herself to wait, she could not resist undoing the metal button of his waistband, then slowly, luxuriously easing down the zip. His penis shot out, wild as a hungry beast. Her fist closed around it, applying pressure at the base, checking and controlling it. He mustn't come yet.

Jason ran his hands over her throat, her shoulders, and finally cupped her breasts. He

8

grasped the nipples between his thumb and fore-finger, rolling and teasing them through the thin silk. Xanthia shuddered, aching with want, every nerve tingling and rushing towards the bud of erectile tissue at her core, the centre of all sensation.

'Show me how you kiss,' she whispered.

He traced the curve of her mouth with one finger, pressing down gently, then bent and captured her lips with his. With a questing tongue, he explored their outer edges, then darted between her teeth, tasting and moistening. Her breath escaped with a great rush and she opened her mouth wide, sucking his tongue into its warm depths. Deliberately he thrust into it, using a jabbing rhythm, thinking that he had conquered her, this marvellous woman who would smooth his pathway to fame and fortune.

He thought himself the victor now, impatient and greedy, hauling her up against him and tearing aside her robe, hands harsh on her flesh, gripping her breasts painfully and pressing her against his erection.

Her eyes flashed open and she glared at him. He was arrogant and spoilt, obviously used to finding women a pushover, so handsome that they drooled over him, no doubt, letting him treat them any way he liked. He little knew that he had found his match in her.

'That's hardly the way to make love,' she snapped, yet her control was slipping, her cleft hot and slick, her body swaying towards his hardness, needing it to fill her, stretch her to the limit. But that wasn't the point of the exercise. 'I really must teach you how to kiss, how to caress. I'm not interested in something that's nothing more than a fuck.'

'What d'you mean?' Jason snarled, stung by her words.

With a tremendous effort of will, Xanthia broke away from him, dropped her robe to the floor and beckoned him imperiously. His jeans had slid down to his thighs and desire weakened her knees at the hugeness of his shaft and the size of his balls, tight, not pendulous, at the point of releasing the pressure building up at the base of his spine.

'Follow me,' she breathed and walked slowly towards the ornate bathroom. 'Class begins right away.'

Jason, grabbing hold of his jeans, his cock still stiff as a lance, almost climaxed at the sight of her naked body strolling away from him, irresistibly alluring. He was desperate for relief – those rounded buttocks, the slit between them, that slim waist and those long thighs acting like a magnet, drawing him after her. He could think of nothing but plunging his penis up to the hilt in her warm, wet passage. The idea almost pushed him over the edge, but by concentrating hard on the unpleasant demands of his bank manager he managed to subdue the throbbing ache.

The bathroom was decorated with joyous exuberance, lined with turquoise Islamic tiles, the square sunken tub rimmed with gilt, the taps of solid gold. Glass shelves ran along one side, filled with bottles and jars of unguents and scented oils from all over the world, some worth hundreds of pounds an ounce. Jason had never seen anything more extravagantly luxurious, and could hardly believe his incredible luck.

'I've made love to many pretty boys,' Xanthia purred. 'But none as lovely as you. Now, you have to learn how to pleasure me. A massage first, I think.'

She would not tolerate a man gratifying himself and leaving her frustrated. This had happened frequently in her youth and she had vowed, then and there, that when she became powerful it would never happen again. She crossed to the couch situated in an alcove and lay on it, face down.

'You're so beautiful,' Jason exclaimed, standing over her. 'What d'you want me to do?'

'Take off your clothes,' she ordered. 'Then chose one of those creams from the shelf and rub it all over me, from the tips of my toes to the nape of my neck.'

He removed his shoes, wriggling out of his jeans and whipped the tee-shirt over his head. Xanthia, head to one side on the bench, looked him over with the eye of an expert. He was perfect. His back, arms, legs and chest swallowed with muscles as hard and smooth as rocks, and the skin that covered him flowed flawlessly. She liked the height of him, the length of him, the insistent firmness of his flesh, the splendour of his cock. It was perhaps, one of the largest she had ever seen, and her knowledge of the male member was extensive.

Her eyes were on a level with it as he stood close to the massage bench. He had not been circumcised, and this pleased her. She preferred her men unaltered, liked to watch the rounded knob emerge from the wrinkled foreskin as it became engorged. Jason's was that, all right – engorged, red and eager, a single bead of moisture dewing the bulbous tip.

But he must learn to school his impetuosity and wait. She stretched languorously, motioning him to drop to his knees beside her and apply the scented cream, then asking, 'Have you ever given a massage?'

'No. You'll have to tell me what to do,' he replied, voice thick as he fought to control the

11

urge to throw himself on her, force her down and ram into her warm vagina until he spent himself. But she was too important a woman to offend. 'Teach me,' he added humbly.

So she did, and it was a fascinating lesson. She taught him how to spread the cream firmly, with long, slow strokes, trailing from the back of her neck, across her shoulders, down her spine, along her sides, just brushing the swell of her breasts.

Once, she had to reprimand him, saying with a serpentine curl of disdainful lips, 'Not so hard! You aren't trying to scrub the stain from a carpet!'

'I'm sorry,' he muttered, strung out on the rack, finding it impossible to concentrate with the feel of her satiny skin under his palms, an electric tingle shooting though his groin, that untamed animal springing up from his crotch every time it brushed against her as he worked.

She rolled over, subjecting him to the full glory of her body, eyes half-closed. Soon his fingers would find her creamy wetness, part the pink folds and massage the gnawing ache between her legs. He tipped a little puddle of oil on to her breasts and began to knead them gently, concentrating on the brown points of her nipples. He was entering into the spirit of it now, beginning to appreciate the sweet torment of having to wait for his release. Languidly, she reached out and took his shaft in her hand, feeling it jerk.

This was too much for his control. 'Now, please!' he begged. 'Let me put it in you!'

'Not yet,' she cautioned, smiling. 'I'm not ready.'

She spread her legs apart, then took his head in her hands, guiding him down to her mound. Jason understood what she wanted; he had attempted cunnilingus with one of his girlfriends but it hadn't been a success.

12

The perfume of her juices filled his nostrils, her nails digging into his scalp, drawing him ever closer. He tongued the insides of her thighs, and she lay as if in a trance, her skin unbearably sensitive. Her grip became tighter, more urgent, as she guided his mouth to where she needed to feel it most, shuddering as his tongue flickered over her clitoris before settling down into a light, moist, delicious rhythm.

Xanthia felt herself centering, felt her whole being focusing on that burning spot which he was manipulating so skilfully. He's a natural, she thought, while coherent thought was still possible. What a find!

'That's lovely – lovely!' she grated, arching her back, pushing up against his mouth, hardly conscious of her own voice, giving herself up to her pleasure of her forthcoming orgasm.

One wave – two waves – three – four – each was more intense than the last. She was soaring higher, higher. Roughly she clutched at Jason's hair as he knelt between her legs. The feel of his tongue was so right, the pleasure acute. She peaked with a cry of ecstasy, shaking and jerking, aware, at the very last moment, that Jason had pushed his fingers into her vagina, giving the ridged walls something to grip as the spasms rolled through her.

The blood was roaring in Jason's ears, pulsing in his cock. Pressing Xanthia down on the couch he entered her in one sharp thrust. She was completely wet now and, raising her pelvis slightly, she drew him into her, feeling the rockhard length of his rod filling her entirely. She convulsed around him, wanting to prolong and savour the delicious feeling, but her tightness sent him spiralling over the edge, and he came in a flood.

13

He collapsed across her, burying his face in her neck. When he looked up at last it was to find her green eyes smiling at him, her red lips curved in an indulgent smile.

'I'll give you eight out of ten points for that performance,' she murmured, shifting from under him, stroking his back, her fingers slipping down the length of his spine to his buttocks. 'And as you're such a keen student, I think we'd better try again. Don't you?'

Chapter Two.

SUNLIGHT CREPT THROUGH the drapes at the window, early morning light that touched the serene interior of the bedroom, the cool white walls, white carpet, white bed. It trailed impudent fingers over the occupant sleeping beneath a floral patterned duvet, caressing her cheek, her loosened dark brown hair, her eyelids.

She sighed, and flung an arm across her face to shut out the day. No use. She was waking now, coming to herself, facing what had to be faced. She was alone in the double bed. Charles had gone for ever. There was a sense of loss, but no pain.

This had worried her at first. It worried her still, that lack of emotion, that blank within her. But then, there had been no emotion in their marriage – almost an old-fashioned wife as an adjunct to his career, and she an up-and-coming interior designer seeking a father figure who would help her to become established.

Charles Logan had been the bridegroom of whom her mother had heartily approved.

'He's wonderful, darling,' she had exclaimed after Heather had shown her the diamond and ruby engagement ring. 'So handsome and distinguished, and a famous architect, too. Aren't you lucky? I've always hoped you'd marry some-one like him. He reminds me so much of your father.'

I suppose that's why I was attracted to him, Heather thought, turning on her back and clasping her hands behind her head. All my other attempts at relationships were disastrous. And since I've been widowed the sharks have gathered, those men eager to console me – Charles's friends, or so they claimed. To get away from them I went back home to my mother, seeking peace.

Peace? Hardly, Heather concluded, not with her mother constantly fussing. Being widowed so prematurely had put Heather in an untenable position, mother taking over when her resistance was low, insisting that she stay with her until she adjusted, imagining that she was prostrate with grief. She wasn't. I'm wicked, she thought.

All this tiptoeing around got on her nerves. Kind, of course, Oh yes, they were all so kind, treating her like an invalid. She missed Charles, naturally, but if there was the slightest stirring of emotion it was one of relief.

She recalled their wedding night, spent in a mock-Elizabethan monstrosity outside Chester, scene of the elaborate reception that had cost a fortune. One of a chain of similar hotels catering for the *nouveax riches* who had more money than taste, its designers had mixed periods with an insouciance that had offended the knowledgeable Heather.

Thus the newly-weds had occupied a Victoriana bridal suite, with a four-poster bed, and gilded furniture, all reproduction, as much a sham as her marriage. No love-match, as they had both been aware, though she had harboured idealistic notions.

16

A romantic, head stuffed full of dreams, she had been accustomed to losing herself in the world of books. She had thought that marriage would fulfil these dreams. It hadn't. Charles had been drunk when he came to bed. She had realised that he drank a great deal but not that he had a problem. Bathed, perfumed, arrayed in a transparent Janet Reger nightgown and négligé, hair streaming across her shoulders, she had awaited him eagerly, fear and desire warring within her.

'Phew! I've had a teeny bit too much to drink,' he had said, falling across the mattress. 'Never mind. Got to do the business.'

He had opened his silk dressing gown and, to her astonishment, held his balls in one hand and, with the other, started to massage his penis. Even now the memory excited her. She stirred restlessly, opening her nightgown to below her breasts, fingers tingling at the contact with her own skin, touching the nipples so that they stood up, firm and erect, that mysterious and alarming ache invading her thighs.

She had looked at Charles's cock as he played with it, pushing down so that the rounded tip appeared from under the crinkled folds of flesh, the head growing, reddening, pulsating. He had seemed oblivious to her, concentrating on making his organ thicken and extend. She had wanted to hold it, to take it between her lips, caress and suck it, nipples prickling, moisture dampening her throbbing vulva.

Her brain had whirled with fantastic desires: she wanted to have him suck her, too, explore her crotch which was aching persistently, to feel his fingers teasing her nipples, his lips biting at them – his hands everywhere, seeking out the most secret places of her body.

17

'Charles,' she had breathed, almost whimpered, moving towards him. Her hands had reached out, touching the tip of his cock, feeling him jerk and gasp.

Giving her no chance to relish the feel of his member, and not stopping to prepare her in the way she wanted, he had simply rolled her on her back, parted her thighs with his knee and, bracing himself, guided it into her opening. It had hurt, she remembered that vividly. Her pleasure had vanished and pain had taken over as he had strained against her. Too excited by his own handling of his tool, he had come almost immediately, collapsing heavily on her.

Then, and here she hated him and the memory of him, he had pulled away, turned on his side and slept instantaneously. Not only asleep, but snoring, the crowning insult.

Now Heather's desire cooled as it had done on that night in Chester. Her disappointment had been acute – disappointment, baulked desire, resentment and indignation.

This had set the pattern of their life together.

I've never been satisfied, she mourned, rising and going to the en suite bathroom and running the shower. I don't think I can be. I'm frigid. Boyfriends told me that before I met Charles, and it must be true for I never once enjoyed sex with him, or with myself or anyone.

Desperately worried, she had consulted manuals which had suggested various methods for female arousal. Masturbation seemed a favourite, but every time she tried it, she would recall her mother's stern command, issued when she was a child and curious about her sexual parts. Mother had caught her, knickers down as she examined her small hairless crevice, and said, 'Don't touch youself there, Heather. It's rude.

18

Nice little girls never play with themselves.'

Mother who must always be obeyed – that stern, beautiful, ever elegant martinet who controlled her family in a clever, manipulative way, an expert in emotional blackmail.

Heather showered and then dressed slowly, choosing a cream silk and lace brassière, briefs, and matching suspender belt. Her body came alive as her fingers brushed it, a warm, wanton animal longing to be stroked. After turning her stockings inside out, she pulled them on and up her legs. Standing before the mirror, she turned round, looking over her shoulder to see that the seams were straight. Her reflection showed a slim woman with a narrow waist, gently rounded hips, the firm buttocks outlined by lacy panties.

She wished there was a man there to see her, not any man, of course, but one of those heroes from the books she loved to read – someone gallant and appreciative who wouldn't be drunk when he came to bed, but eager to caress her into ecstacy before thrusting his mighty phallus into her.

As she watched herself through half-closed lids, her tongue came out to run over her lips. This desire of hers was becoming ever more urgent, tormenting her so that she could think of little else, yet had no idea how to successfully relieve it.

But there was someone who might help her and, remembering her luncheon date, she completed her toilet hurriedly. People who had accepted her as Charles's wife and, later, as his widow, had no idea of the lustful yearnings concealed beneath her calm exterior. She appeared cool and aloof, always attired in superbly cut, expensive clothes which were deceptively simple in design. This morning was no exception: her Chanel suit of linen and silk weave in a natural shade, her blouse of tan shantung, her court shoes of Italian make with low heels.

The lightest dusting of powder, the merest hint of mascara and beige shadow, a creamy pink lipstick and she was ready to go, her long hair pinned up tidily. No jewellery, save the gold band on her wedding finger and a pair of tiny diamond stud earrings.

Soon she was in her car, driving through the deserted country lanes to link up with the motorway which would take her to London. And her heart seemed to beat in time to the turning wheels as she thought about the man she was going to meet. His name was André Beaufort and he and Charles had been friends for years, though his line of business was quite different. André had something to do with the film industry, Heather wasn't sure what.

He was a bachelor, dark-haired, sophisticated, always immaculately turned out in hand-crafted suits, tailored shirts, Gucci shoes and the most costly accessories. Near Charles's age, he seemed much younger, his body whipcord lean, honed by regular visits to an exclusive sports' club. His mind was keen, a clever, witty individual who had been much on the scene since Charles met his doom in that fatal car accident. Heather had appreciated his attentions, the unobtrusive way in which he had kept an eye on her, always there at the end of the phone if she needed to talk.

And now she *did* need to talk, but not of Charles. André was the one person in whom she felt she could confide. As she approached Richmond and Hammersmith Bridge, the traffic thickening on every side, so she was screwing up her courage to confess the one thing which she wanted to do above all other. She wondered if she would have the nerve to say to him over lunch in some ultra-smart restaurant,

'André, I've never had an orgasm. I want you to teach me how to come.'

André Beaufort lounged in the director's chair of his executive suite in the palatial complex facing Chelsea Harbour. It was a humid summer day, the sun glittering over the Thames. Far below the massive windows, barges filled with sightseers chugged lazily past, while guides pointed out historic landmarks.

Business completed for the morning, André's thoughts turned to his midday assignation. He was taking a woman out, and a faint smile tugged at the corners of his mouth as he remembered her. Heather Logan. Ice-cool Heather. An innocent, or so she appeared – a girl who needed help to recognise her full sexual potential. His body hardened at the idea that he would be the one to show her. Not only him. There would be others involved, too.

He buzzed the intercom and, within seconds, his personal assistant entered. He watched her progress across the shining marble floor. She was blonde and plump, voluptuous even. Not one of those fashionable stick-insect females. He always thought of her as Rubenesque, the kind of model sixteenth century artists loved to paint. Lusty, earthy, all bouncy boobs and curvaceous buttocks.

'Has the studio faxed us, Julie?' he asked, but idly. This was not the reason he had summoned her.

'Yes, sir. The script is ready, the casting done, and they're waiting to go into production. The director wants to see you as soon as possible.'

Julie could feel herself blushing. André always made her blush, had done so from the first time she had entered his presence, a rookie secretary needing a job. He had given her a chance and, that night, when lying alone in her tiny flat, she had thought about him. Her fingers had wandered down, touching the fringed rosy petals of her labia. She had felt herself becoming loose and pliant and wet, spreading that wetness silkily over the sensitive nub that commanded her touch.

It had been her boss's face she had see as she had stroked her clitoris, rousing and inflaming it. André who was so swarthily handsome, with a kind of sombre beauty that was almost poetic. God, that mouth of his! The upper lip was firm, hinting at impatience with incompetence, but the lower was full and sensual. In her imagination, he had knelt before her, urgent as he opened her thighs, his phantom tongue desperate to lick that vital spot, making her writhe with need.

Even now, standing before his glass and chrome desk, she could feel the cotton gusset of her knickers dampening at the memory of this and a hundred other nights when he had been her fantasy lover. Her breasts seemed to swell within the D cups of her brassière, sensitive nipples in direct communication with her clitoris.

'I'll phone Aaron later. Now, will you reach down that file from the top shelf, Julie?' he said, and watched her as she obeyed him, mounting a set of library steps.

She was wearing a short, tight skirt, her shapely ankles, rounded calves and knees on view as she reached up on tiptoe, stretching for the file. Her skirt rode higher, till he could see the tops of her stockings, the black suspenders, an area of white thigh, the edge of her panties straining against her large, luscious backside.

Andre's eyes slitted, the fullness of his lower lip more pronounced as he waited for her to climb down and place the file on his desk. He caught her perfume as she leaned over. An expert in such matters, he recognised it as *Ysatis* by Givenchy. This, mingled with her pungently sexual female smell, was enough to rouse him to fever pitch.

He controlled himself, never one to hurry pleasure. It should be savoured to the last drop. He flipped open the file which contained an album of professionally executed photos. 'These are of Charles Logan's wedding, when he married Heather,' he said, aware of Julie's heavy breasts beneath the thin striped blouse rubbing against his shoulder as she leaned nearer under the pretext of viewing them closer.

'I remember. You were his best man,' she breathed, her voice unsteady. 'So smart in your morning suit and top hat.'

André gazed steadily at the pictures. 'She was a lovely bride.'

Jealousy gnawed at Julie's gut. An upsurge of hatred engulfed her, as it always did when he praised any other woman. Somehow, she looked upon him as hers, ridiculous she knew, but there it was. She was his aide, his confidante, *au fait* with every aspect of his complex business affairs, or so she thought. In reality, there were many areas of both his life and career which André discussed with no one.

He had been deliberately denying her for months, knowing precisely how she felt about him, sensing that she might well fall in love. He was not a conceited man, but couldn't fail to be aware of the devastating effect he had on women.

He had been seduced by a lady of fifty when he was sixteen, and remembered her with gratitude. She had taught him how to make love, uninhibited in her desires, giving him a detailed knowledge of the female anatomy which helped him with the subtleties of foreplay. This, more then anything else, had endeared him to his subsequent mistresses.

He outstripped other equally handsome and virile men by being an expert lover. He genuinely liked women, finding them so much more interesting than men. They instinctively recognised that, with André, they would be not be left unsatisifed, burning with frustration and turning to dildoes or their own fingers for completion. It was as if he breathed out the promise of sexual gratification through his pores.

Now he felt the time had come to end Julie's misery, though conscious that in some ways it might increase it. His motive was not entirely selfless. Looking at the photos of the lovely, aloof Heather had made his prick stand up. If chafed against his trousers, hot for immediate release.

'Lock the door, Julie,' he commanded.

Her eyes switched to him, mouth red and wet, echoing the colour and wetness between her legs. His erection was apparent and she gasped, running to obey him. She couldn't believe it. This was the moment she had dreamed of, prayed for. He must love her, mustn't he? Just for an instant the words 'Mrs André Beaufort' flashed across the screen of her brain.

She was more naive than André had bargained for. His intention was to fuck, not marry her. But first, she must do as he asked.

'Quickly,' he said huskily. 'Come here. Kneel before me.'

Julie been expecting kisses, mouth to mouth contact. The kisses were to come all right, but not on the lips. She dropped to her knees, unsure of what he wanted, but beginning to understand,

24

memories of pictures in the sex magazines she devoured rapaciously rising before her. Oral sex. She had read about it, thought about it, now she was about to experience it.

'Do it,' André growled, his eyes heavy-lidded, feeling her willing fingers touching him through the fabric of his slim-fitting slacks, tentatively at first, then becoming bold, clasping his stiff organ.

Her mouth moistened, tongue licking her lips, blue eyes dreamy, trancelike. She reached up, unfastened his waist buttons and, grasping the tag of his zipper, gently eased it down. André slumped low on his spine, head resting on the back of his leather-padded chair, lids lowered as he watched.

His trousers gaped. Beneath them her fingers encountered silk boxer shorts, dipped inside the fly, caressed the black pubic hair and closed in on his shaft, freeing it from restraint. His groan of pleasure excited her beyond all reckoning. She was trembling, her loins on fire, sobbing with excitement. He clutched at her hair, guiding her mouth till her lips brushed the tip of his cock. He held her there, held her still.

'Don't move,' he whispered. 'Make me wait. I don't want to come yet.'

She obeyed by instinct, learning fast. Her fingers grasped him, rubbing gently, her breath warm on his damp red knob. Then, under his sure, steady guidance, she took it between her lips, slowly, carefully going down, down till she could feel it pressing against the back of her throat, almost choking her with its size.

She wanted him inside her, filling her with that giant length. It was too much for her to take, only a part of it had gone in. But she could take all of him in the natural way, she was sure, aching to ride on it, to feel him penetrating her eager, tight-muscled sheath.

André could feel his will and energy concentrated on his cock, her mouth, the strong working of her fingers bringing him near to the edge. This was the closest he ever came to losing control, the moment when he gave himself over to the tumult of orgasm. He relaxed, felt the force gathering, tearing through him in a great wave. He pressed hard at the base of his tool to prevent the explosion. Then he looked down at Julie, working so earnestly to bring him pleasure. He seized her fingers in his own, then held her chin still.

What a patient woman she was, how loyal, deserving of better than giving him a blow-job and getting nothing in return. He withdrew his penis from her mouth. She started, stared up at him, worried in case she had been clumsy or hurt him in some way, with her teeth perhaps. Now he would send her away, the magic lost. Her eyes filled with tears.

'That's lovely, Julie,' he said, gently reassuring. Then, rising to his feet, he drew her up with him, bending to bury his face in the sweet-smelling neck, adding, 'But this will be better, for both of us.'

Closing her eyes, willing herself to be still, she waited to see what he would do next. André's lips travelled from her throat to her ears, blazing a trail of fire. And his hands cupped her breasts, lifting, testing the weight of them. The breath slid from between her lips in a rush, her spine curving, breasts thrust up to meet his fingers that now circled her nipples through the blouse.

An electric shock stabbed into her womb as his lips skimmed over her face, then fastened on her mouth. She ripened beneath his touch, her whole body melting against him. His tongue probed as she opened wider, wanting to absorb, almost eat him. As he explored the warm, welcoming cavity, so his fingers unbuttoned her blouse, slipped inside, pushing down the brassière and rolling a thumb across the bunched pink tips of her nipples.

Unable to stop herself, Julie fastened her thighs around his, grinding against him, rubbing her crotch up and down, needing his touch between her legs. He responded at once, a hand beneath her skirt, lifting it high, then tearing aside the fragile barrier of her panties. She opened her legs slightly as he brushed the fair hair on her mound, one finger slipping between her sex-lips, dipping it into the wetness seeping from her and spreading it over her hot, needful clitoris which was protruding from its tiny hood.

Julie moaned and trembled as André settled down into a steady rhythm, not boringly so, varying it, now hard, now featherlight, but never moving away from the seat of her arousal and fulfilment. Julie's eyes closed and her head fell back. Then, with a sharp cry, she climaxed, clinging to him, gasping with joy.

He moved swiftly, lifting her so that she lay on her back across the desk, legs falling open on each side of him as he rammed into her with the force he knew she desired. The feel of her wet, contracting vagina was too much for him. He spilled himself inside her with a violent convulsion of pleasure.

At that moment the phone trilled. Automatically Julie fumbled for it. 'Yes?' she said, amazed at how normal her voice sounded.

'Mrs Logan is in the lounge,' replied Cynthia of Reception.

'Tell her I'll be right there.' André withdrew from Julie, grabbed a a handful of tissues from a box in the desk drawer and loped into the bathroom, holding on to his trousers.

He dried himself on a fluffy black towel and zipped up. A quick flick of the comb through his hair and he was ready, so cool and urbane when he returned that Julie could scarcely believe that he had been vigorously humping her only a few moments before.

André shot out a darkly furred wrist to consult his platinum Blancpain. 'I'll be in later, Julie. Must put through that call to my bankers. I've been working on a proposal to finance Sirius Pictures, but you can think about it, too.'

'Yes, sir,' she replied, clothes straightened, once more the efficient aide, while inside she was breaking up.

When the door closed behind André, Julie traced his steps into the bathroom and, fishing about in the laundry basket, found the towel he had used to wipe his genitals. Sitting on the toilet-seat she clutched it to her, searching for the white stains, breathing in the salty smell of their mingled juices that clung to it like a steamy miasma. Pressing her face into it, she began to cry.

'Well, Heather?'

'Well, André?'

They smiled at each other across the table, having reached coffee and liqueurs and that time when they could dispense with small-talk and get down to the nitty-gritty.

The restaurant was as modern as could be, on the ground floor of the complex, where a huge, glass-domed area occupied the centre, with exclusive boutiques and eating places branching off on either side. It glittered. Everything was fearsomely expensive. A Mecca for the rich and those who hoped to be rich. Marble, stained glass, a positive jungle of exotic potted plants. Chinese food, Indian dishes, Thai, Malaysian, Japanese – anything was served in those pricy restaurants except, perhaps, plain English fare.

This was not Heather's first visit. Several times of late she had met André there, so convenient for him to take the elevator from his penthouse office and glide down to entertain. He could even have a drink or two, if he wished, though this was seldom when he was working.

Now she looked over at him from beneath her lashes, and questions hovered on the edge of her tongue. He was sensitive to something different about her that day, an ambience which he could not quite fathom.

'Did you get that commission from Lady Jenny?' he asked, providing her with an opening.

'I did. She was thrilled with my ideas for her Bath mansion. She's American, as you know, and hasn't much idea about the decor for an eighteenth-century house. She's given me *carte blanche* to buy whatever I like for it – curtains, wall-paper, antiques.'

'Congratulations. When do you start?' He wanted a cigarette, but had recently given up smoking, taking himself off to a group that dealt with nicotine addiction. It was working, but one of the disadvantages was that his hand felt awkward without that slim tube between its fingers.

Heather sat back in her chair and crossed her slim legs. He heard the sibilance of sheer stockings rubbing against one another, and thought about the tops resting so close to her sex. The craving for an Abdullah became stronger. Maybe he could take up cheroots?

'In a month or two,' she answered evenly.

'Lady Jenny isn't in a hurry. I have till December to complete. She wants to throw a New Year's Eve party there.'

'Are you going on vacation?'

'I've nothing planned. I'd like to get away, of course.' Heather's grey eyes darkened to pewter, and her mouth set. 'Mother is driving me mad!'

André chuckled. 'Is she now?' He could well believe it, knowing the Honourable Mrs Miller-Saunders rather well.

An admirable person in every way, much more fun to be with than her daughter imagined. But then Diana Saunders had always taken parenthood very seriously, and devoted herself to Robert and Heather.

'I'm worried about her, André,' Diana had said to him on the phone only last night, unbeknown to Heather. 'She's so rigid, if you know what I mean. Too much control – hasn't broken down and cried for Charles once. It's not natural. As for this obsession with working! Well, you know what I think about that. I'd rather see her married again, if it was down to me. I have offered to pay for her to go abroad on holiday. Mary would love to have her in Boston – that's her aunt, my married sister. She'd have a super time with those delightful American men. They are positively charming. But no. She won't hear of it. Talk to her, André, she may listen to you.'

Ah, my dear Mrs Miller-Saunders, if you only knew what I have in mind for your beloved offspring, he thought cynically, as he watched Heather – and waited.

She was a delight to look at, and he had always found her so. He was glad that the red and white checked table-cloth hid him from the waist down. If not she might have noticed the bulge in his slacks caused by looking at those gorgeous legs and wondering how it would be if she were to slip off a supple leather shoe, stretch out one stockinged limb and nestle her toes in his groin.

As if aware of something in the atmosphere between them, Heather wriggled slightly, feeling the silk wedge of her briefs drawn tight against her mound. Her wide-spaced eyes rested on André's face, admiring his pronounced cheekbones and aquiline nose, and that wonderful, mobile mouth. He was handsome indeed, reminding her of Mr Rochester in *Jane Eyre* – dark, mysterious, powerful. Yet he was her friend, her good, understanding friend. I must speak to him, she thought, the colour flushing her cheeks giving her skin a delicate, cameo-like luminosity.

'I suppose it's early days yet, but have you found another man?' André asked quietly.

'No.' She was suddenly terribly shy.

'My dear, why are you so afraid?' He leaned forward, reaching across to clasp one of her hands, this action doing nothing to ease the discomfort in his balls. Thank God he'd had the foresight to bonk Julie!

Heather was trembling, both with the sudden stab of fire that engulfed her at his touch and his astute recognition of her inner turmoil. 'I've always been afraid,' she whispered breathlessly.

'Of men?'

'Of myself – of what I am inside! You don't know me. No one does. I have these images – these desires – and I don't know what to do about them.' There, it's out, she thought, and was glad.

He drew back, signalled to the waiter to pour more coffee, then said, 'Didn't Charles satisfy you?'

She shook her head, blushing furiously, her eyes fixed on her cup. 'No, he did not, but I never knew what it was I expected or wanted.'

All around them she was aware of the tinkle of cutlery, the chink of glasses, the rise and fall of cultured voices and the occasional burst of laughter as lovely women and their elegant escorts sat at table. Sunshine fell through the massive plate-glass, casting coloured patterns across the brown ceramic tiles. Outside London sweltered, but air-conditioning kept the restaurant at an even temperature.

Despite this, Heather could feel the sweat trickling down her back, between her breasts and in her armpits. She was betraying Charles and his memory, and conscience dubbed her the blackest of traitors.

André withdrew his hand, placed his elbows on the table, steepled his finger together and stared at her over them. 'Charles wasn't a good lover?'

'No, I guess not, though I had nothing to compare him with. My only lovers had been dream ones from the pages of books.'

'You were a virgin when you married?'

'Yes,' she murmured, and had the distinct and darkly stirring impression that André resembled a confessor – cool eyes, a level voice, an impersonal set of questions. *Forvive me, Father, for I have sinned!*

'And since?'

'There's never been anyone.' She took a deep breath, then added: 'You'll find it hard to believe in this day and age, but I've never had an orgasm.'

Though André kept perfectly still, her words caused him to experience the most intense spasm of physical pleasure. He almost came. He clenched his thigh muscles, swallowed hard, then replied, 'Never? You've never even played with yourself?'

'Never. I've read books about it, but can't do it. I wish I could. I know I'm missing out on something tremendous and don't feel I'll ever become a real woman unless I can get over this sexual block.'

'You're right, Heather. One must learn to appreciate the erotic if one is to grow.' His voice was very serious. 'You are lovely, but like an innocent schoolgirl, which is fine in its way, but hardly suitable for you any more. I'd like to discuss this in depth. There must be some reason why you've not experimented, if not with men, then with yourself. Masturbation's an ideal way of discovering what one needs.' He smiled deeply. 'I've heard it said that sexual intercourse is a poor substitute for it, but each to his or her own.'

'I must admit that I didn't get much enjoyment sleeping with Charles,' she answered and, before she knew what she was doing, had poured out the story of their wedding-night, her disappointment, her longing for a virile lover to bring her to completion.

'I knew he drank,' André commented when he could get a word in edgeways. 'Alcohol's a soporific. It deadens sexual response, often making men impotent, if they take too much. A little is fine to get rid of ones inhibition. But the Greeks said, 'Nothing in excess.''

'I've never done anything in excess.' She wore a worried frown.

André laughed and patted her hand. 'Then it's time you dipped a toe into the water of sin. Or should I say a nipple, or even your pussy.'

Every word he uttered was disturbing her more – her labia were wet, her briefs clinging to her. She could not stop watching his mouth, dreaming of having it feeding on hers, or sucking her breasts or tonguing her forbidden parts.

'I don't think I can. Where can I go to find a lover? Who can I trust to teach me?'

André's long, strong fingers were idling with his gold fountain pen in lieu of the longed-for cigarette. He turned it this way and that, deep in thought, then said, 'I know the ideal person to advise you. You need a break, and I'll introduce you to Xanthia Delaney.'

A puzzled frown drew her wing-shaped brows together. 'Who is she?'

'A friend of mine. She owns a house in Cornwall, a beautiful old manor which she runs as an exclusive hotel. It offers a special, very unusual service.'

'I don't understand.' Heather's eyes were bright with suspicion.

'Trust me, darling.' He urged, his own eyes shining, so deep and dark that she could feel herself drowning in their hypontic depths. 'I'll ring her and make arrangements. What say we go next weekend?'

'You'll come with me?'

'Of course.'

Much later, when even Julie had left the office and the sunset-streaked evening was throwing gold bars across the river, André lifted the receiver and pressed a sequence of numbers.

A rich, melodious voice answered him and he smiled as he visualised her, the one and only love of his life. 'Hello, Xanthia,' he said. 'And what are you doing at this precise moment, darling? Playing havoc with someone's hormones?'

'How did you guess? André, how lovely to hear you.'

'I'm coming down on Friday, bringing Heather Logan with me.'

'Ah, yes, the Ice-Princess. So, you've managed

to swing it, have you?'

'I have indeed. We're going to give her a wonderful time. I'll tell you what she needs when I see you.'

'Do that my sweet. I can't wait.'

'Neither can I.' André replaced the receiver on its rest and walked to the window, a slow, musing smile settling on his features.

Chapter Three

THEY STOPPED AT the Jamaica Inn on Bodmin Moor for lunch and, over a simple meal of grilled lamb chops, baked potatoes and fresh green salad, Heather began to relax. A sense of holiday pervaded her. It was as if she was shrugging off a tremendous burden – no mother to bother about or please, no responsibilities.

André was driving his powerful Bentley, a vintage machine of which he was intensely proud. To be behind the wheel gave him the same sense of domination as when he was penetrating a woman. When he picked Heather up at her Chelsea flat, she had been surprised to discover that he wasn't alone. His secretary, Julie Foster, was with him. Plump Julie of the 42 D-cup bra, high complexion and nervous manner. Heather could not know of the conversation that André had had with her in the office last evening.

'How would you like to come to Cornwall for a few days, Julie?' he had asked casually.

The colour that mounted to her cheeks, the hope that sprang into her adoring blue eyes confirmed his fears. She was falling hopelessly in love with him.

'That would be wonderful, Mr Beaufort. What

is it? A business trip?' Julie had been stunned. He was actually inviting her to go away with him!

It must be something to do with work, she had thought quickly, putting a curb on hope which, in her experience, could only lead to disappointment. He'd want her to bring along her lap-top computer, wouldn't he?'

André had smiled, regretting his lack of control the other day, yet all too aware of her fleshy body beneath the skimpy skirt and blouse, remembering how gauche she had been, those untried lips working on his member. It had swelled at the recollection.

'It's not work, Julie,' he had assured her, resisting the urge to bend her over the desk and push his tool into her, using short, sharp thrusts. 'I'm taking Mrs Logan to visit a friend, and I thought you might like to come along.'

Julie's heart, which had been banging like a drum, had seemed to sink down into the pit of her stomach. Jealousy had nipped her with sharp fangs. She had been furious at his interest in the intelligent, beautiful young widow.

'I don't understand,' she had started to say when he stopped her with a gesture.

'Mrs Logan's been stressed out for some time, and Xanthia Delaney's exclusive guest-house is the ideal place for her to relax,' he had answered, while Julie had watched, fascinated, as his slim, aristocratic fingers played idly with the sophisticated executives' toy that stood on his desk – a precisely balanced chrome and black Newton's cradle.

Tock, tock, went the balls, swinging to and fro. And Julie's heart had echoed the sound at the vivid memories of his testicles rapping softly against her perineum as, legs raised and wrapped round his waist, she had lain there as he rode her.

'Why have you invited me?' she had whispered, feeling as if her very life depended on his reply.

André had risen to his feet, suave and elegant in his perfectly tailored suit. He had come close and Julie had drawn in a deep breath, her senses reeling at the smell of *Joop!* eau de toilette, coupled with that raunchy odour which was all his own.

He had reached out a gentle fingertip and lightly touched her left nipple. Unable to help herself, she had groaned and closed her eyes, head tipped back, lips parted, ravenous for his mouth.

'Julie, my dear,' he had said softly. 'Like Mrs Logan, you take life too seriously. I want you to learn how to enjoy yourself, and realise that love need not be confined to one man – or woman, for that matter. You'll be taught how to do this at Tostavyn Grange.'

Now the two women fenced around one another during lunch, both wary but for different reasons. Julie resented Heather, while she, who had hardly been aware of André's secretary in the past, wondered why he had brought the woman along. But as soon as the Bentley left the inn and purred through the winding country roads, they became less tense. By the time they wheeled into St Austel they were ready to accept the adventure, soothed by the master magician, André, who was well aware of and amused by the undercurrent of emotions filling the car.

Leaving the port, where the light had a special dazzle over the water and gulls circled overhead, they drove through charming villages with thatched cottages straggling down the narrow central streets. André, almost as interested in history as Heather, pointed out the churches, their towers decorated with projecting gargoyles, and the Celtic crosses on the greens. The country was flat, the scrubby trees compelled to bend in one direction by the powerful wind gusting from the omnipotent sea.

Heather sat up in the passenger seat, straining against the belt that crossed and separated her breasts. André, hands on the wheel, glanced sideways at her, noting how her pointed nipples raised her white tee-shirt, her long, slim thighs displayed to advantage as the thin brown and cream cotton of her palazzo pants fell away from them.

He wanted to see her in the briefest of denim cut-offs, so tight that the central seam dug into her crease. He imagined the merest wisp of dark pubic hair showing as she moved, the shorts scooped up over her buttocks at the back, her bare inner lips pressed into the warm leather seat. Later, he promised himself. Xanthia's going to enjoy training this one.

They reached a gorse-covered headland where the sea hissed and rumbled against the rocks far below, and still the road wound onwards, finally running into a wood and breaking at a stone gateway. The gables and latticed mullioned windows of the lodge peeped over the moss-grown wall. Ancient it might be, but the entrance was equipped with electronic sensors. It swung open soundlessly and the Bentley passed through.

Heather had the most curious sensation as the gates closed behind her, an intellecutal as well as physical thrill. It was as if she was entering an enchanted world far removed from ordinary, everyday life – a world where anything could happen.

The house stood at the end of a tree-lined

avenue. It had all the stateliness of a Georgian country seat. Heather appreciated the architecture, the size and grandeur. The Bentley rolled to a standstill before a flight of wide stone steps topped by a Corinthian pillared portico. At once the great front door was flung wide and a woman came running down to meet them.

'Xanthia, darling!' André leapt out and she was in his arms, looking up into his face and laughing as they rocked with pleasure at seeing one another. He kissed her full on the mouth, his hands sliding under her short chiffon wrap to cup the pert cheeks of her backside revealed by a minuscule bikini.

'Hello, André.' She had a low but richly carrying voice, this woman with her almost bizarre beauty.

He released her and opened the car doors for Heather and Julie.

'So, these are my new guests,' Xanthia exclaimed, and enfolded them in turn in a perfumed embrace. 'Welcome to Tostavyn Grange!'

She was the most extraordinary creature Heather had ever seen, with a mane of wet, tangled gypsy locks and vivid green eyes. As slim-waisted and keen-hipped as a boy, yet the breasts that pressed against Heather's with an intimacy she had never before experienced from a woman were large and perfectly shaped, the dark areolae of her nipples showing through the damply transparent robe.

'I came straight from the pool when I heard the car,' she explained, on a husky note. 'I love swimming and sunbathing. Don't you? So deliciously idle and decadent.'

Her legs were exquisitely brown beneath the diaphanous garment, and her feet were bare –

long, slender feet with delicately arched insteps, the nails painted with glittering gold enamel. Everything about her suggested casualness and carefree abandon, except for the antique emerald earrings that flashed against the dark fall of her hair. These reminded Heather of gems she had seen featured in a sale at Christie's.

Did she wear them while swimming? Heather reflected. And concluded that she probably did. It would be her style – eccentric – individualist – a creature of impulse.

Her senses stirred at Xanthia's closeness, and she pondered on who she might be. She gave the impression that she was a lady, living in baronial splendour. That wonderful house, the perfectly tended formal gardens and Capability Brown landscape, were the epitome of graciousness, and yet her nudity, and that wildness that hung about her like a wicked aura, spoke of a hedonistic attitude to life.

Xanthia exchanged an amused glance with André, squeezing Heather's waist and saying, 'Come inside. I'm dying to hear all about you.'

Julie, hesitant, followed them up the steps. She felt over-dressed and out of place, sweating in her ankle-length, flowered River Island dress which she had thought so trendy, until Heather had appeared in those cool coffee shades, and she had been confronted by the near naked Xanthia.

That woman! Julie was thoroughly disturbed by the intimacy with which André had held her, the current that had almost crackled in the air between them. The way his hands had caressed Xanthia's tush! Just as if he was re-establishing possession. Julie was sick to her stomach. Some holiday this was turning out to be!

Xanthia led them across a semi-circular hall decorated with rams' head friezes, and into a drawing-room. Every detail was perfect; the burgundy and silver upholstered wingchairs that flanked the marble Adams fireplace, richly swagged with carved acanthus leaves and bunches of grapes; the brass andirons and fender; the period tables of peachwood; the great priceless Chinese vases on ebony plinths; the lush Persian carpets strewn on the highly polished cedarwood floor.

Heather was accustomed to residing in splendid surroundings, but this went far beyond mere luxury, though never descending into the vulgar.

An extremely tall, hawk-faced Arab servant, dressed in a black caftan and turban, offered pink crystal flutes of champagne. Xanthia took one from the silver salver, subjecting the regally handsome and impassive man to a ravishing smile.

'Thank you, Samir,' she said and, to Heather's utter disbelief, reached out with her free hand and lightly jiggled his balls. It happened so swiftly that she couldn't be sure whether she had seen it or not.

Carrying her glass, Xanthia settled on a chintz-covered couch and crossed those eye-catching legs. In doing so, Heather was granted the merest flash of her area at the very top of her inside thigh, and the tantalising vision of black fuzz – a glimpse, no more. But it was enough to send a flush rising to her temples, while the excitement engendered by Xanthia's familiarity with Samir churned and grew within her.

'Has André explained the entertainments we provide here at Tostavyn?' Xanthia asked, her smile deepening as she noted Heather's confusion, enjoying her covert interest.

'Well, no – not exactly,' Heather managed to reply, seated opposite Xanthia, who seemed to

42

exude a rich flow of sensuality as she beckoned André to join her on the couch. 'I thought maybe I'd swim – ride – or go for walks.'

Xanthia chuckled, a mischief-inspired sound, and lying back amongst the feather-filled cushions, lifted her golden-brown legs and stretched them across André's lap. 'You can do all these things if you wish, but we have something better on offer. André tells me that you read a lot.'

'That's true.' Heather could feel her inner self tightening, moistening, watching the intimate way in which Xanthia was playing with the hair that grew low at the back of André's neck.

Were they lovers? Hot vignettes of them having intercourse, right there on the couch in front of her and Julie, ripped through her mind. Her sex was wet, her nipples brushed by the jersey cotton of her sleeveless top. She glanced at Julie, and saw that she, too, was staring at them, blue eyes bulging, mouth slack and glistening. The idea that she was roused almost beyond endurance added to the heat scalding through Heather's veins. She was horrified to discover that she wanted to touch Julie's enormous breasts.

'When you've been reading, have you ever longed to be the heroine?' Xanthia continued, rubbing one foot up and down André's leg. 'I'm sure you have, Heather. Didn't you wish that you could be Cathy bonking Heathcliff in the heather when you waded through *Wuthering Heights*? Or how about Scarlett O'Hara and Rhett Butler? I remember when I read *Gone With The Wind* being terribly frustrated because Margaret Mitchell didn't describe in detail their love scenes together. Well, Heather darling, I'm about to make your dreams come true. That's part of the service here. Everyone who visits us can play out their most secret fantasies.'

'I see.' Heather stumbled over the words. 'And how do you do this? Does one have to have acting abilities? I've performed in amateur productions, but not for years.'

Xanthia sat up and swung her legs to the floor, giving her a reassuring smile. 'Don't worry about a thing. Leave the practicalities to me. This house is steeped in magic. It has dozens of rooms, and there are buildings at the back – studios, if you like – where any setting can be constructed.'

She stood up, lithe as a panther, moving with the sensuous, confident grace of a woman who knows she is infinitely desirable to both sexes, and revels in it. Julie experienced both lust and ravening envy, looking across at André with reproachful eyes. He avoided them, simply smiling and saying,

'I'm sure you would both like to see your rooms. Samir will conduct you there. We'll meet later.'

'Isn't there any work you want me to do, Mr Beaufort?' Julie squeaked, totally at sea in this situation and hating to see him go.

'No work – not of the kind you're used to anyway,' he said, his voice as seductive as silk. 'Relax, Julie. Stop worrying.'

As Heather and Julie followed Samir through the door, Xanthia pressed her body against André's. 'Come upstairs,' she murmured. 'I want to know more about Heather. And why did you bring that dull Julie person?'

He kissed her lightly, the tip of her tongue darting out to meet his. 'Ah, the devoted Julie. Well, darling, she's getting too fond of me. A victim, if ever there was one – used and abused by men. A love-addict, if you like, getting herself involved in relationships that only bring her pain. We must teach her how to reverse roles.'

Arm in arm, they strolled up the light, airy staircase suspended on lacy ironwork. They paused on the upper gallery, looking back over the magnificent hall. 'Very altruistic of you, my sweet,' Xanthia commented, shooting him an oblique stare from her feline eyes. 'But she won't be able to pay, will she?'

'Materialistic bitch,' he whispered lovingly, teeth nipping at her ear. 'This one will be on me. It'll be worth it to get her off my back.'

'And Heather?' She leaned into him, and they continued walking, stopping only when they reached the huge double doors that led into her private apartment.

'Heather's rich. Charles left her very well off indeed. I want the best for her. This is to be the experience of a lifetime.'

Inside her boudoir, Xanthia occupied a stool before an ornate dressing table, peeled off her robe and removed the bikini top. Her breasts emerged in all their glory. Holding them, she stroked the nipples into erect points, eyes half closed as she considered her reflection.

'She's not a virgin, is she?' she asked, observing André in the mirror.

He stood behind her and she rested her head back, nestling it against his belly, aware of the swell of his cock. 'Technically, no, but she's told me that she's never had an orgasm.'

'Never!' Xanthia found this hard to believe.

He shook his dark head, bending to lick over her bare shoulders. 'Never – so she assures me. She doesn't know what it's like.'

'Never known this—' she took one of his hands and guided it down to where the little triangular strip of spotted material barely hid her mons.

André pushed it aside, staring at the depilated area, cunningly bare so that her mound resembled

45

that of a much younger female, a line of fluff purposely left to compliment the delicate pink flesh dividing it so neatly, dipping down to disappear between her legs. Xanthia gasped and, raising her hips, spread her thighs wide. He opened her vaginal lips, moved position so that he could examine them, finding her clitoris and stroking it. The surrounding area was red now, but the swollen organ itself, protruding from its hood, shone with the hardness and hue of a translucent pearl.

'Not all women are as lucky as you, darling,' he said seriously, watching her reaction as she tossed back her head and moaned, hips straining upwards against his experienced finger. 'You've always liked sex, haven't you?' He was on his knees between her legs now, the thong stripped away, absorbed in his study of her exposed parts. 'Such a responsive pussy, used to masturbation. D'you want me to bring you off?'

'Yes – yes – do it now, André. Now – now – ah, I can't hold it back! It's coming. That's it! Yes – oh, yes—'

Heather's room stunned her with its magnificence and beauty. Large, the lofty ceiling frosted with plaster swagging as elaborate as the icing on a wedding cake, it had tall windows that gave on to a balcony commanding a spectacular view of the garden.

Samir had brought up her suitcase, then retired after instructing her to pull the tasselled bell-cord hanging near the green-veined Carrara marble fireplace if she wanted anything. Heather drifted round this dreamy chamber, in the seventh heaven of delight.

A collector with an all-consuming passion for antiques, she was delighted by the harmony of

46

every item. The four-poster bed with its towering *ciel* was genuine Regency, no fake this. Gently fingering the drapes of apple-green brocade, she could tell by the quality and craftsmanship that these were original. The mystery deepened. Who was Xanthia and how had she managed to acquire such glorious things?

Heather consulted her slim, diamond-studded wristwatch. It was late afternoon and André had said they would meet at the cocktail hour of six. Time enough to unpack, and take a long, hot, blissful bath, but not before she discovered the sound equipment and a range of compact discs.

Better and better! Opera! Her prime passion in music. Soon the velvet voice of her favourite tenor echoed round the room, that amazingly sensual quality of tone that sent chills down her spine, connecting with her loins and darting upwards to her brain.

There were concealed speakers in the bathroom which was off to the right, again in keeping with the rest of the suite. Original Victorian fittings of white porcelain elaborately patterned with cabbage roses, but with the addition of modern plumbing. Soon the out-sized tub was filling with hot water from gold dolphin-shaped spiggots, and Heather had added perfumed oils from the selection on the flowery tiled shelf.

It took her a second, no more, to strip, then she stepped into the warm, scented water, sliding down and relaxing, her head resting against the gently curving side. The bath was certainly big enough for two, maybe more. The music continued to wash over her in waves of mind-blowing sound.

Eyes closed, Heather began to drift, erotic images rising behind her lids. A man sharing the tub with her, perhaps – what sort would he be?

Dark, for preference, no blond macho man with unnaturally developed biceps. She had never been turned on by the Chippendales or Gladiators. She suspected that they were gay anyway – too conceited and dedicated to their appearances to merit a woman's serious attention.

No, her ideal lover would be made up of several parts.

She toyed with the possibility of an android – a creation constructed to incorporate her desires. He would be tall, dark and classically handsome, resembling Lord Byron or a Brontë character brooding over some dark secret. An adventurer like Indiana Jones, but also intelligent and sensitive, appreciating art, literature and music. It would be essential that he sing like an Italian, and have the vigorously masculine and lyrical talent of a Bolshoi Ballet dancer.

Heather smiled sleepily, soothed by the water made smooth as satin by the addition of costly oils. How good it would be to have such a one, switch him on when she needed him, then, once he had satisifed her, unplug him and put him away in a cupboard till next time. No emotional entanglements, no hurt, no quarrels, just pure pleasure and entertainmnent.

The disc had finished. She was almost asleep, but the falling temperature of the water roused her enough to turn on the hot tap. Even the sponge was larger, thicker, softer than any she had seen before. She worked it over her body, filling it and then squeezing the water over her arms and back. Sensuous warm rivulets streamed over her breasts and caressed her nipples into peaks.

There came a light tap on the door.

'Who is it?' Heather called, instinctively covering her breasts with the sponge.

'Xanthia. Can I come in?'

'Yes – I suppose so,' Heather answered uncertainly, eyeing the distance between the bath and her dressing gown that lay across a gilded stool.

A movement, the door closing and Xanthia was perched on the rim of the tub. She took the sponge from Heather and continued the water play exactly as Heather had.

'You like your accommodation?' she asked, one dark brow winging upwards.

'Oh, yes – it's divine. I suppose André told you how much I adore anything old and unusual, and the music is just right.' Heather was aware that her nipples were tip-tilted through the suds, like the hopeful noses of household pets. What were they expecting, the naughty things? To be pampered and caressed? A tingle shot through them and flashed down to her clitoris.

Xanthia had changed into an evening gown of silky black jersey. Its halter top clung seductively to her body and the skirt fell in a tight, straight line to her ankles, revealing strappy gold high-heeled sandals. Every movement she made was calculated to tempt and tease.

'That's good. I'm pleased that you're pleased,' she said, continuing to caress Heather with the sponge. 'I want you to wear something different tonight. Not exactly your usual choice, I think, but bear with me and try on what I've brought along.'

'All right.' Heather wished her hostess would leave so that she might have privacy to get out of the bath, yet there was a dark, salacious pleasure in knowing that Xanthia had no intention of moving and was about to watch her emergence.

She did, feasting her eyes on Heather's lovely body, touching her only once, and that was to skim a pointed fingernail over one rosy-brown

49

nipple. It immediately bunched in response to that perfunctory contact. Heather reached for the enveloping robe, wrapping it tightly around her lusting flesh, and holding a fold in front of her like a shield. She padded into the bedroom, leaving wet imprints on the carpet.

Xanthia followed her, a secretive smile lifting her crimson lips. How like André to find such a treasure. This was an exceptional girl. She seemed so vulnerable, virginal even and yet, like him, Xanthia recognised the promise of a passionate sensuality which, when unleased, would know no bounds.

Those nipples, for instance, what hungry little beasts they were. Don't worry, my dears, Xanthia addressed them mentally, you'll soon be given your fill of delicious sensations.

She was not very interested in Julie. Let André continue her education if it amused him to do so. Though she did agree that it was high time Julie stopped being the victim. Xanthia had plans for her, and so did he.

Indicating the gown spread across the bed, 'Try it on. See if it fits,' she suggested, willing Heather to discard the towelling robe.

Their eyes met, Xanthia's deep, magnetic pools into which Heather could feel herself being drawn. It was not only her allure and ravishing beauty. There was more. It was as if she exuded sex through every pore of her body. It seemed the most natural thing in the world to submit to her. Heather let the robe fall, shivering in the sudden chill as the air danced over her damp skin.

Xanthia's breathing shortened, seated on the bed beside the exquisite garments she had brought. André's right, she thought. This girl has a rare quality, worthy of careful consideration and development.

'You're very beautiful,' she said, the look in her eyes sending the colour flooding up to Heather's cheeks. 'Is it true, as André says, that you've never known what it's like to come?'

'Yes, that's right.' Heather was ashamed of the admission, wanting to hide, to put on the dress.

Xanthia's hand closed on her wrist, preventing her, keeping her there naked. 'I'm glad, sweetheart,' she whispered. Her juices were flowing with the desire to stretch Heather on the bed, prise open those still virginal thighs, stimulate her vagina and massage her clitoris until she exploded in an earth-shattering orgasm.

Her first! How glorious to be the one in initiate her.

But this was not to be her privilege. 'Excite her. Prepare her.' André had instructed. 'That's all. We want her strung out and eager – then it will be done.'

'Can we watch?' Xanthia had said as they lay on the bed in her boudoir, her hand stroking his cock until it became fully erect again, never getting enough of him.

'What do you think?' he had teased, caressing the soft fullness of her mouth with his tongue.

They were to be voyeurs, and this was one of Xanthia's favourite pastimes, second only to masturbation. As they watched, so they, too, would receive sexual satisfaction. There would be hands, lips, pricks and wet pussies belonging to other watchers, all eager and willing to perform and be performed upon.

'Ah, Heather, you'll achieve your goal tonight,' Xanthia promised in that low, dusky tone. 'It's wonderful, darling.'

She drifted a hand down the girl's spine, a light touch, causing such mayhem within Heather that she forgot to be shy. 'You mean that you'll find me a lover?' she gasped, leaning forward and

51

supporting herself on her hands.

Xanthia chuckled, and let a finger come to rest on Heather's soft and hidden bud. 'Not necessarily. We want you to have the finest orgasm possible, and this isn't usually achieved by male penetration.'

'No?' Heather rested against her weakly, blushing at that intimate contact, wanting more. 'But I thought – believed that this was the ultimate pleasure.'

Xanthia could feel her own arousal starting, a pulsing in her clitoris. It ached to be rubbed. She knew that she could disobey André and take Heather now. She wanted so much to introduce her to every delight, slip a hand over her mound, a finger between the innocent, eager labia before toying with that awakening bud. She longed to taste Heather's juices, bury her face between those white thighs and suck each pink fold and that clit which would palpitate for release, until finally the girl screamed in ecstatic completion.

But no – this was not to be – she would not be the one to take Heather's innocence.

'Time to dress,' she said. 'I'll help you.'

'Is this all there is – this one garment?' Heather stared at the strapless gold lamé tube.

Heather stood up and gathered it against her. 'You need nothing else, except a mask and cloak.'

'No underwear?'

'Only these black silk stockings and garters.'

'Not even panties?'

'Panties are a drag. I don't wear them, unless I feel they'll increase my excitement by having someone rip them off. It depends on my mood. You'll learn to enjoy their absence, too.'

'Isn't it rather cold in winter?' Heather stepped into the gown and Xanthia went round to zip up the back.

'Stop being so practical,' she laughed. 'You've to forget all that while you're here, and for ever after, I hope. You've a lot to learn, but this will come later. Now, sit down and spread your legs.'

Xanthia positioned herself between Heather's knees and rolled on stockings which were so sheer that they resembled grey mist. To adjust the garters, it was necessary to push up the gown with which Heather was shyly trying to conceal her naked sex. From where Xanthia knelt she could look at the dark wedge close up. The urge to separate the pink cleft, to massage Heather's labia with smooth, rapid movements was almost uncontrollable. As it was, she could feel moisture filling her vulva, dampening the sparse hair, and spreading along every fold and secret nook.

Damn you, André, she thought, feverishly. When Heather's finally taught to climax, it had better be good!

She stood up, put out a hand and raised her, then adjusted the ruched bodice which was cunningly boned to stay in place and push the breasts high. They swelled above it, bare almost to the tips. The skirt clung to the waist and hips then fanned out into a fish-tail at the hem. It was provocative and Heather, catching a glimpse of herself in the mirror, was astonished at the transformation.

Xanthia took up the silver-backed hairbrush and stroked over Heather's long locks till they resembled a silken curtain falling halfway down her back. The sensation of it caressing her bare shoulders was enjoyable, soothing, and the image in the mirror was of a fairy-tale princess, not herself at all.

'Not too much make-up, only your lips which must be painted red,' Xanthia said, replacing the brush on the shining surface of the heavily carved dressing-table. She slid her arms round Heather from behind, her palms testing the size of her breasts. 'Everyone will be masked tonight.'

'Masked? Why? Is the theme that of a Venetian ball?'

Xanthia nodded. 'That's right.' She removed her touch from Heather's pleasure-hungry nipples and took up the elaborate and fantastic mask that lay on the bed.

It was perfectly constructed, a replica of a face, oval, beautiful, androgynous, chalk-white with blue and pink flowers painted on the cheeks and brow. The gilded eye-slits slanted upwards, the left one emerging from the spread wings of a fuschia and gold butterfly, the upsweeping antennae forming exaggerated lashes.

Xanthia tied it at the back of Heather's head, and she thought as she stared at her reflection, I'm no longer me. Only the mouth was her own, the mask pared away over the lips, to continue down across the chin and jaw – Heather's mouth, glistening, crimson.

'You're lips are beautiful,' Xanthia murmured, 'Ready to consume whatever's on offer – food, drink – or private parts longing to be sucked into passionate completion.'

The next instant, she was carefully arranging the voluminous black silk domino over Heather's shoulders. The hood covered her hair, its stiffened cloth-of-gold frill lined with another of pink gauze and trimmed with ribbons and bunches of artificial flowers. It framed the dead-white mask that peered out from it – ghostly, alarming, blood-chillingly fascinating.

'Now you're anonymous.' Xanthia stepped back the better to view her. 'Heather Logan has gone, replaced by whoever you want to be. Enjoy.'

Chapter Four

IT WAS THE most extraordinary gathering that Heather had ever attended. The vast reception room glittered with light from the chandeliers whose diamond facets radiated prismatic colours. These hung at regular intervals from the ornate ceiling where Venus wantoned naked with two amorous Cupids, their cocks at the ready, while a collection of snow-white doves preened or mated around her.

The scene was repeated again and again in large, gilt framed mirrors of Italian design, and in the panes of the massive french windows draped in blood-red damask. Their pelmets were a fine example of *trompe-l'oeil*, the lifelike plaster designs imitating the hue and folds of the curtains. Even the thick, twisted cords and fringes were an illusion.

Standing there uneasily, a Margarita in one hand, Heather wondered if the people milling about or gathered in chattering groups admiring one another's bizarre costumes were equally unreal. Expressionless, sinister – human faces replaced by the blank stare of masks. Each person was shrouded in a black cloak like her own, but between the folds she could see that they were dressed as Renaissance princes or cardinals, whores and queens, apes and fauns, some got up to look like Egyptian deities and some like medieval troubadours.

On wore a Medusa wig, while another flaunted an enormous feathered headress. Some were fully clothed, some half naked, but, as far as she could see, their costumes were discreet. But then, she reflected, people might think this of herself, not realising that beneath the lamé gown she was bare. Should the skirt be lifted, the twin globes of her tight bottom would be revealed to all.

Those viewing from the front would see the dense, crisp hair part-concealing the deep cleft between, those rosy, succulent lips swelling in anticipation. She wanted to do it – wanted to expose herself – was frightened and repulsed by her own driving need.

'You're disappointed? You were hoping to be present at an orgy?' someone whispered in her ear.

She turned, but could not make out the features of the man in the purple velvet mask beneath a tricorne hat. No matter: he couldn't disguise his voice.

'I had no expectations, André, she said. 'This reminds me of a scene from *Amadeus*, when the young Mozart thinks he sees his dead father. Why is it that masks are so alarming?'

He chuckled, and threw a fold of his cloak back over one shoulder. Beneath it he wore a parti-coloured Harlequin costume, the extremely close-fitting tights accentuating the impressive protruberance at the apex of his thighs. As Heather watched in fascination, so this appeared to be growing even larger. Was he wearing a jock-strap, as ballet dancers do? she wondered. If so, it must be strained to the limit.

His hand was on her bare arm, a feathery touch that raised the down all over her body. 'Ah, the masquerade! The Venetian élite revelled in such gatherings, using them as a means by which to indulge in illicit liaisons. Masked, one is incognito. One can perform any act with a willing partner, and there's no comeback.'

'Will this happen tonight?' She was torn between flaming desire, fear and apprehension.

He laughed again. 'This is only an introduction, a way of insuring that our guests lose their identity. They'll eat well, drink a lot, but not too much, before embarking on the serious quest for pleasure which is their sole reason for being here. No one exchanges surnames or addresses. You can use your given name, if you want, or assume another, as fanciful as you like. It's up to you. No one knows anything about the other's business. No couples pair off – not yet, at any rate. By the end of their stay? Who knows? Though bonding isn't encouraged.'

'Are they all guests?' Heather found it difficult to comprehend that there could be so many rich, though lonely souls anxious to fulfil their cherished dreams.

'Only a couple of dozen, including yourself and Julie. The rest are helpers, dedicated to making people happy.'

'They do it for love?'

'For love – and for money, but I can assure you that they enjoy their work.'

He offered her his arm and she rested her fingertips on it gingerly as they started to stroll through the room towards the buffet tables. Even the footmen wore masks, though silk stockinged and pumped in full livery. Engaged for their height, the shape of their legs, and the proportions of their genitalia, they had on white powdered wigs, sky-blue coats with massive silver aiguillettes and broad silver seams down the front and round their waistcoat pocket flaps. Tasselled garters clinched the knees of their tight crimson breeches, emphasising those bulging calves. Not only these were bulging. Each specimen was exceedingly well endowed.

'Impressive,' Heather remarked as she viewed this mini-regiment of studs.

'Aren't they just? Hand-picked by Xanthia, in more ways than one. She obtains a great deal of satisfaction in receiving a man's ejaculation in her cupped hand. I've often watched her do it. As for taking it in her mouth, she simply adores the taste of semen, says it has the salty flavour of beef cubes – though I can't agree with her there.'

Heather's belly clenched, her cheeks flamed and she was thankful that she was masked. Was André hinting that he, too, had let a man come in his mouth? But he was heterosexual, wasn't he? She went cold as she realised how little she knew him.

There was still time to turn and flee. She imagined running back to her room, changing into one of her reassuringly cool and restrained Jil Sander outfits, flinging her belongings into a suitcase and phoning for a taxi. She could be on the night train back to London in an hour, this surging lust that André's words evoked no more than a nightmare from which she had escaped.

A further Margarita and the waves of panic receded. André helped her to refreshments from the wide variety of delicacies. She paid silent tribute to the sumptuous panorama of the long table, its linen white as a sheet of freshly fallen snow. Scintilating cut glass; candles providing an infinity of intersecting lights; the mouth-watering odours wafting from beneath the shining domes of serving dished whetting both appetite and curiosity. Every item was temptingly displayed, calculated to titillate the palate of the most jaded gourmet.

Ornate épergnes spewed forth cascades of perfumed flowers, orchids predominating. Heather found herself gazing at the pronounced stamens, the tight buds, the pink through the crimson folds. Everywhere she looked there seemed to be sexual connotations. Bronze statuettes of naked nymphs supported piles of fruit – dusky purple grapes whispering of assignations in Italian vineyards on hot afternoons, yellow bananas the length and shape of a well-developed phallus, suggestive of delights other than mere consumption, peaches with the damp dawny bloom of a young girl's pubis.

What's happening to me? Heather wondered in alarm. And wanted to ask this of Julie, who had recognised and descended on them. André greeted her coolly, then wound his hand up under her skirt. By the tiny moans of pleasure escaping from Julie's lips, it was obvious he was slipping a finger in and out of her vagina.

Somehow Heather's glass was always brimming, even though she was sure she was downing the Margaritas. Her head was reeling. 'That's enough, I think,' André said, his voice coming from a great distance.

Everything was hazy, the whirl of colours, the drift of costumes, the mingled scents. On a raised platform beneath an arch, a group of musicians were playing Ravel's *String Quartet in F Major* – sensual, yet light and frothy as ocean foam. This was followed by six boys singing madrigals – cherubs in white robes with frilled collars.

'They sing like angels,' Heather murmured, leaning against André.

'Indeed their voices are celestial,' he agreed, 'but they're of that age when the testosterones are rampant and erections a more or less permanent feature of their existences. A miserable, over-sensitive period of one's life when one doesn't know how to cope with that huge thing constantly demanding relief. It's like an alien, with a mind of its own.'

'I always wanted to be a boy, and own a nice big plonker instead of my tiny little button,' Julie confessed drunkenly, the words tripping her tongue.

A thread of laughter weaved through André's voice. 'It's a very important button, and to be envied for its easy stimulation.'

Julie was riven with frustration because he had roused but not satisfied her, having withdrawn his hand at the vital moment, leaving her hovering on the edge. She needed to hurry away to the ladies' room, there to lock herself in one of the cubicles and caress her clitoris into orgasm.

She had the desire to tell André everything, holding nothing back. There was nothing really wicked to tell, only the terrible burden of past torments – a father she could never please, faithless lovers, broken promises, brief moments of joy atoned for by hours of misery. He'd promised to help her. To ease her suffering heart that was constantly being broken. She looked to him for guidance.

The music died down and a woman occupied the platform, holding up a hand for silence. Her face was covered by a green mask, she wore a crested feathered helmet, a green, topless gown, breasts taut, nipples gilded, and an enormous peacock's tail that fanned out behind her.

'Welcome, my friends!' Xanthia cried, her voice ringing over the assembly. 'Welcome to Tostavyn

Grange! The night is young, but in an hour we shall go our separate ways. There's work to be done, your first taste of the delights available here.'

Cheers and thunderous applause. She left the stage, disappearing through the purple silk curtains. 'Time to go,' André said and, leaving Julie to her own devices, guided Heather to the hall and grand staircase. 'Xanthia's told you what to do next?'

'Yes.' Her voice was a whisper.

Back in her room again, Heather pressed her hands to her temples, eveything dipping and swaying. I've had a drop too much, she thought. All I want to do is go to bed, alone. But she knew she must follow her instructions.

It was easy enough to slip out of the cloak, untie the mask and drop the single garment she had worn. Wearing so little was exciting, her skin responding to so much freedom. André had told her that the secret of eroticism was surprise. She frowned as she pondered on this, for her, entirely new concept.

He had said that the shock of discovering that the tiaraed vicereine at a Court function was wearing no knickers and the viceroy had, beneath his dress-uniform, a satin suspender belt and black stockings, was extremely erotic. So was being observed masturbating, or watched when copulating with a member of whichever sex happened to turn you on at the moment. It was also stimulating to catch others at it.

'Surprise! Shock! The unexpected! These are supremely exciting,' he had insisted.

'Not for me,' she had prevaricated. 'I believe in love, a couple dedicated exclusively to one another, with no one else – no unfaithful encounters – a pair bonding for life.'

'Give yourself time. It will be amazing what peculiarities you discover in yourself, once the magic door is unlocked. More often than not, the real person hidden beneath the everyday façade makes itself known during fantasies.'

Well, that's about to happen to me, Heather thought, walking naked to the mirror, gazing at her body as she ran her hands down her slim flanks, skimming over her flat stomach, her fingers tracing the line of dark hair slicing across her mound. She trembled at her own touch, aching, hot and needful. Her inner self was beginning to ripen and unfurl.

I want – *I want!* Heather almost screamed. I don't know what I want!

Do as I've told you, she could almost hear Xanthia's melodious voice whispering, then you'll get to find out what you need. I've promised you, haven't I? Trust me.

On the bed lay a plain silk blouse and skirt, an outdoor jacket, beige stockings, court shoes, a pure white garter belt, panties and brassière. Heather put them on, fingers made awkward and fumbling with eagerness and alcohol. It was a tasteful ensemble, very conventional. But there was one important difference.

The satin and lace panties were open crotched and, as she stood in front of the mirror and lifted her skirt, she could see the crisp fronds of pubic hair puffing out of the slit. Unable to resist, she pulled the opening tighter and her outer lips protruded, surrounded by that hairy frill. She could feel the moisture seeping from her vulva and resisted the urge to open the split-crotch wider and dip a finger into that dewy pool. She was aroused, her own sweet, sexy smell rising warmly to her nostrils.

A rap on the bedroom door startled her. She

tugged down her skirt and went to open it. A young man stood in the passage outside, a very handsome young man with long brown hair, a square face and level brows. He smiled at her with light hazel eyes, and said, 'Are you André's guest?'

'That's right.' Heather blushed as she wondered if he was to be the one to demonstrate the meaning of pleasure.

Such a wholesome young man, wearing a baggy three-piece suit of speckled tweed, a Polo Ralph Lauren by the casual excellence of the cut. A brown roll neck sweater and brown brogues completed his attire.

He was a member of the county set. One associated him immediately with Irish wolfhounds, shooting sticks, and willowy, stragglyhaired girls in fearfully expensive designer berets, long thin skirts, skimpy cardigans and thick woollen stockings worn with clumpy shoes.

He smiled and his face lit up, the most charming smile she had ever seen. 'They are ready for you. I'll show you the way.'

The way to what? The thought sprang unbidded into her head. The way to orgasm? I wouldn't mind him as a teacher, though he looks rather raw and inexperienced.

She picked up her calf-leather handbag and followed him along the dimly lit corridor. Their feet made no sound on the dark red carpeting, and neither of them spoke, though he smiled at her encouragingly. Down a short flight of stairs, along a further passageway and then he stopped outside a door, saying as he rapped softly on it, 'Here we are.'

It swung open noiselessly and Heather stepped inside. The young man did not accompany her and the door closed as if by an invisible hand.

She found herself in an ante-room. It was small, circular, with a glass cupola set among blue and gold stars. The pillars were of wood painted to imitate marble. There were portraits of beautiful women on all sides, executed in the Edwardian era when it was considered quite proper, in the name of art, to depict naked girls in imaginary antique settings – Greece, perhaps, or Ancient Rome.

Heather noticed a further opening concealed by an arras. Close by stood another handsome man, this time of Italianate colouring, dressed in a sleek evening suit. He smiled across at her, and held back the tapestry, nodding his head to indicate that she was to pass through.

She did so, then stood stock-still on the threshold, barely aware of the curtain dropping back into place.

This room was furnished in that baroque, overblown style beloved of earlier eras, verging on the Gothic. Dark drapes, heavy dark furniture – a wealth of settees, couches, daybeds – a plethora of mirrors – yet there was more. It was very much overdone, and reminded Heather of lithographs she had seen of high-class brothels of the period.

Under the twinkling gasoliers, six women disported themselves, dazzling, beautiful, eclipsing every other marvel of this place. Black velvet ribbons circled white throats, wasp-waisted corsets constricted figures, breasts spilled over the tops of bodices. Long legs in black stockings, diamanté-studded garters, lace-trimmed drawers, high buttoned boots. Feather boas draped the overstuffed chairs. Cartwheel hats, aquiver with silk roses and ostrich plumes, were tossed on tables.

Heather drank in the tableau, her widening

eyes taking in what her slow wits did not at first perceive. The women ignored her, ignored each other, totally absorbed in pleasuring themselves.

One lay on a chaise-longue, her legs stuck out straight in front of her, breasts rearing up as she tweaked the nipples into points. Another occupied a chair, knees wide open and hooked over the arms on either side as she ran her fingertips over her sex. A third stood spread-legged before a pier-glass, pelvis thrust forward, eyes feasting on the image of her crotch as she rubbed it vigorously.

A fourth was on knees and elbows on the floor, hind-quarters rising and falling rapidly as she used both hands to massage her swollen clit. A fifth sat on a stool, legs spread as she smoothed oil into her labia and caressed her vulva. The sixth and last reclined on a bed, a hand-mirror held between her gaping thighs, watching her bud expand and grow as she toyed with it.

They were oblivious to anything except their gratification of themselves, by themselves, for themselves.

Heather could not tear her eyes away, waves of heat laving her loins, which felt heavy, as if all her blood was rushing to settle between her legs. Those women – she saw what they were doing – one, in particular drew her attention, the girl on the chaise-longue.

She was taking her time, stroking her exposed genitals in leisurely fashion. Her legs were wide apart, and Heather could see that deep cleft, the flushed lips, the swollen bud at the top. No completion yet for any of them, apparently. Heather felt like cheering them on – eager to see what happened at the very end.

But then a woman entered from another door at the rear of the room. She was attired in a dark blue nurse's uniform, complete with starched white apron and cap.

'This way, madam,' she ordered Heather. 'The doctor will see you now.'

Doctor? Heather didn't recall there being any mention of a doctor. These are games, remember? she told herself sternly. Sex games for adults, based maybe on infantile fixations. Doctors and nurses. Didn't children sometimes play this in order to satisfy their curiosity about each other's sexual organs? Heather never had, and now giggled a trifle hysterically as she wondered if she had been a deprived child. Deprived, when it would have done her more good if she had been depraved.

Knees weakening, nerves strung out like bowstrings, she followed the nurse.

She was in a sterile, white-walled apartment. It was dominated by a narrow, hard, consulting-room couch. A big man in a white coat, the lower part of his face hidden by a surgical mask, stood up as she entered. There were four other people there.

'My students,' he explained, his voice deep and cultured.

He was handsome, silver-haired, a finely-built man with a quiet, thoughtful air and beautifully manicured hands. His keen blue eyes regarded Heather over the edge of the mask. He studied his notes.

'I see here that you've never climaxed. We'll have to do something about that, won't we, my dear?'

Heather nodded shyly, though her excitement was intense. Every nerve in her body seemed to be aflame. From the outer room she heard cries. The women were achieving their aim – cries of pleasure, cries of joy. They were coming. She wanted to come most desperately, her senses sharpened by everything that had happened to her since her arrival at Tostavyn Grange.

'Remove your jacket,' the doctor said, and one of his helpers hung it over the back of a chair. 'Now then, slip off your shoes and lie on the couch.'

She did so. It was high and he helped her. 'Relax,' he said pleasantly. 'You're going to thank me later.'

The room was softly lit, and for this she was grateful. 'I shall talk as I work,' he said. 'Explaining to you and to my students what is happening to you or about to happen.'

Heather lay back and closed her eyes. She felt the warmth and weight of the doctor's hands on her breasts. Her heart was racing and her breath had caught somewhere in her throat. A tingle moved along her skin, crawling, prickling, eager, settling in that place between her legs. His right hand cupped her left breast, squeezing gently, his thumbnail scratching across the nipple.

'The breasts are extremely sensitive to touch,' he lectured in a matter-of-fact voice. 'This is to be remembered in the successful arousal of a woman. Men's nipples, too, are responsive, but we're concentrating solely on the pleasure of the woman. D'you like that, my dear?'

'Yes, oh, yes—' Heather could hardly speak.

'How does it make you feel? It will help my students enormously in their research if you describe your sensations at every stage.'

Her breasts jutted like supplicants towards his hands, insistent as the nipples hardened beneath his fingers. 'It feels wonderful – hot – aching, and that ache culminates at the top of my opening. Unbutton me, please,' she begged.

'You want my touch against your naked flesh, is that it?'

'Yes. I want that more than anything. Oh, please hurry!'

He nodded to one of the nurses, and she slowly, carefully, began to open the buttons of the silk blouse, slowly, slowly, one by one. Heather's eyelids lifted. She wanted to see the doctor's eyes as the blouse floated away from her uptilted breasts and ripe reddish-brown nipples, leaving them naked to his gaze. They smiled down at her, the rest of his face hidden.

'Good girl. Now I'm going to stroke and suck them. Like this—'

He pushed up the mask and took each in turn into his mouth, sucking and nibbling and using his tongue. She shivered, squirmed, her hips rising involuntarily. He withdrew his lips in order to continue speaking.

'She's already aroused. It is time to progress further or she'll become impatient, fret about it, lose the impetus to sweep her to her climax. But we'll still go on satisfying those breasts. I want two of you to stand behind her head, and continue caressing her nipples while we examine her genitals.'

Heather lifted her hips and someone, she wasn't sure who, pulled down her panties and put them aside. Her skirt was pushed waist high. The doctor adjusted the flexible lamp so that its spot focused over her pubic area.

'The most important of the female sex organs is the clitoris,' his calm voice rolled on. 'It's the only organ in the human body designed exclusively for pleasure. So why has it been neglected? For make no bones about it, this delightful nub of erectile tissue has been woefully neglected – by men, at any rate. Many don't even know it's there. Ask your average man where the clitoris is and he'll either say he's never heard of it, or won't be able to give you an accurate answer as to its position. Yet it is a tiny bundle of nerve endings, more sensitive and reponsive to stimulation than its equivalent in the male – the penis.'

'Is it like a penis, sir?' asked one of the students, a man, as it turned out.

'Something like. It has a little foreskin, a tiny hood – but it doesn't eject fluid. I'll show you.'

He leaned forward, parted Heather's legs and moved his hand along the length of her thigh. He patted the prominent swell of her pubis, rubbing the soft fur. Next he trailed his fingers across the lips of her sex. Heather sighed deeply and her legs fell apart. He stroked the skin between her stocking tops and her mound, the delicate touch making her moan. Then she felt two of his fingers holding back her labia, opening her fully, his middle finger wandering up the tender cleft towards the quivering point.

'Oh, doctor!' she whimpered. 'I ache inside. What are you doing to me?'

'You want more?'

'I'll die if you don't continue.'

'Good. That's good,' he murmured. 'She's so beautiful there – soft, high and beautiful. Look at how the lips part, first the outer then the inner. See the silken-smooth wet aisle. Note how the mucus membrane thickens and changes colour. Observe the clitoris, that nub at the top of her labia. It's swelling, engorging. A wonderful organ, its stalk rooted firmly far below the surface, actually attached to the pubic bone. And hers is large, I've never seen a finer one. Take a good look, and then I'll start to stimulate it.'

His words stoked Heather's fire. She felt proud of her clitoris. He said it was large! He was about to touch it!

She was tense. Waiting – waiting – never in her

life had she wanted anything as much as she did now. Smiling, the doctor rested one finger on her bud. At once her whole body was filled with fiery sensations, every nerve vibrating as if he had flicked a switch. Her hips jerked, pressing against that knowing digit. He began to rub gently, smoothly, regularly, until her clitoris reared up victoriously.

'It's already hard,' he continued to lecture in that same, even, pleasant voice. 'Come closer. D'you see it?'

The knowledge that they were staring at her pleasure point increased Heather's frenzied excitement. She rolled her pubis against that wonderful finger, and its touch became feathery, teasing that lusty little organ.

She began to moan, a tremor of excitement flowing along her thighs and through her belly, tingling in her spine. The nurses kneaded her nipples, circled them, tickled them, measuring their movements to the doctor's, till it seemed that she had three clits, each encouraging the other to scale the heights.

The doctor's finger sank into her vagina in order to wet it and spread her juices. She moaned louder, and he carefully located that fleshy pearl again, continuing the magical, slow, slippery massage that eased backwards and forwards across it. Not a boring, repetitive stroking, but varied, sometimes light, sometimes hard, easing to one side momentarily when the tension became too acute on so tender a spot. But he always returned to where she craved the friction most, on the enlarged tip.

'Tell me what you're feeling, my dear,' he asked, so kind and considerate that she was about to fall in love with him.

'I can't explain it,' she panted, her heart

thudding furiously. 'I don't want to talk – just to experience. Oh, it's so nice! So good! There – touch me there – not so hard – stroke it – coax it—'

'She doesn't need the aid of oil to grease her,' he said to his pupils on a satisfied note. 'See the moisture running from her vulva? This is the best lubricant of all, supplied by nature but often lacking if a man doesn't excite his female in this way. The clumsy lover can hurt his partner if he penetrates her while she's dry.'

Now Heather began to understand what men feel when they spew forth semen in their orgiastic delirium. The waves carried her up the painful, precious slope, rising higher and higher. She uttered the short, sharp cries that heralded her entrance into the enchanted territory, then she stilled, held in sudden pre-climactic silence.

'She's very nearly there,' she heard the doctor saying. 'We are honoured to be with her during this first orgasm. See how still she is. Eyes closed, breath coming in gasps. Now, I think – now is the moment—'

She wanting nothing to interrupt this wonderful ascent as the doctor and his helpers brought her closer and closer to her ultimate goal. Up and up, breaking in sharp releases, little peaks of pain and pleasure, till she felt herself lifted to the skies on the greatest feeling of joy she had ever known.

Her head snapped back, her body half rising and, at the very moment of climax, though never for an instant neglecting her clitoris, the doctor slipped two fingers into her quivering vagina, her muscles clenching on them in a series of sharp spasms. Glorious moment as she came off into ecstasy!

In a flash she shared the madness for which men and women risked their lives and reputations. They paid for it, intrigued for it, killed for it. At last it was clear to her. She collapsed on the couch, eyes closed, head thrown to one side, her body still shaking, the hot feeling subsiding, leaving a wonderful oasis of peace and release.

The doctor moved his hands to her breasts, not lingering, but coasting lightly. 'Did you enjoy that?' he asked.

'Oh, yes! I never thought – never dreamed—' She stirred, smiled up at him and at his four helpers who stood around, congratulating her as if she had just run a gruelling race and won a gold medal. She felt as if she had, too. 'How soon can I experience it again?'

'So eager?' he said with a laugh. 'You'll be ready now, I dare say, but this time we'll do something extra, shall we?'

'I want the same treatment,' she demanded. 'You must rub my clitoris – play with my nipples – do it as you did before.'

Her nipples received their fair share of attention, her clitoris was petted and encouraged to stand up again, and once more she took the heady rollercoaster towards climax. This time, the two women who acted as nurses raised their skirts and caressed their own sexual organs, while the men unzipped their flies and brought out their cocks which they proceeded to rub energetically.

The doctor, once Heather had climaxed again, straddled the couch, reared above her and plunged his tool into her. It was huge, thick and red, and she felt at first that she couldn't possibly take all of him. But she was so wet, so swollen and expanded that he sank in till she could feel him prodding deep within her. Suddenly he gave a great cry and flooded her passage with a hot spurt of semen.

There followed a lovely period of oblivion,

when Heather slept or maybe imagined that she slept, but somewhere out of timeless night she heard Xanthia saying, 'Now you're a woman, my dear. Wake up. Tell me how you liked it, though I watched your wonderful performance.'

Heather roused, stretched, found herself no longer on the couch but back in her own room. How did she get there? It was strange, for she could not remember anything after the doctor had removed himself from her.

Groggily, she pulled herself up against the pillows. 'You watched me?' she whispered, aware of a slight soreness between her thighs, and the sticky wetness of juices trickling from her opening.

Xanthia sat facing her, clad in a loose silk robe. 'Oh, yes – André and I didn't want to miss a moment of your initiation. There's a security camera high in a corner of the consulting room. So you pleasured several people at the same time – yourself, the doctor, his helpers, and the voyeurs. That's what life is all about at Tostayn Grange.'

As she talked, Xanthia dwelt on the memory of what had taken place not so long before. On the screen in the adjoining room she had watched Heather writhing on the doctor's couch, while André worked her love-bud, unknown hands tweaked her nipples and Jason, positioned behind her, had thrust his shaft into her anus. It had been an electrifying experience.

'Haven't you tried to bring yourself off yet?' she asked quietly, her eyes bright as she considered the girl's disordered beauty.

Heather was no longer an Ice Maiden, hair tumbled about her bare shoulders. She had lost her shyness, ignoring the fact that the sheet had slipped off, exposing her body. Was it Xanthia's imagination, or did Heather's skin have a special lustre, nipples darker, her breasts fuller, her labia more pronounced, after just one session?

'I've been asleep. You woke me. I've had no time to masturbate,' she answered levelly, even though desire surged through her loins as she pronounced the forbidden word. She needed to climax again, and soon.

'Let me see you do it,' Xanthia urged. 'I'll show you how. Nothing beats a leisurely frig. Sometimes I don't want to share it with anyone.'

'There's something I don't understand,' Heather began.

'Fire away. What is it?'

'Well, I was led to believe that a woman climaxed when a man penetrated her.' Heather felt freed – orgasm, so long denied her, had liberated her. Now she could talk about it, discovered that she wanted to talk about nothing else. It was that important.

'A misapprehension put about by men,' Xanthia replied with conviction. ''My implement is so huge and important that you can't possibly enjoy yourself if you don't have it in you!''

'What about the G-spot?' Heather clasped her arms about her raised knees, asking questions that had bothered her for years.

'A theory spread by another man, Ernst Grafenberg. It's even been named after him.' There was a dismissive, impatient note in Xanthia's voice. 'He maintained that there was a small area on the back wall of the vagina which, he claimed, could create orgiastic feelings if stimulated. How the hell did he know? Did he have a vagina? Or was he simply envious of the clit, and resentful because it functions beautifully without a man anywhere about?'

She opened her robe, sliding her hands over

74

her nude body, cupping and bouncing her breasts, lingering lovingly on the nipples, thumbs revolving on them in unison. She gasped with pleasure, saying, 'Even talking about clits makes mine hot up. It needs attention desperately. I can feel it drawing, almost clenching. I've got to touch it.'

Heather, watching, found that one of her own hands had moved to her breast, palm on a hardened nipple. The other went down to her crotch, her finger finding her centre, applying tentative pressure. She felt it carefully, proud as she recalled the doctor's comments about the size of it. By gently pushing in, she could feel its stalk. Probing further, an examination which caused a wave of intense feeling, she was aware of how deeply it went, attached way back on her pubic bone.

'That's right,' Xanthia encouraged, her tongue creeping out to moisten her lips. 'Try it that way, if you want. Give it a hard, sideways rub. Make it stand up and beg for more.'

As she spoke, her fingertips were working on her own bud, inflaming it with tiny slaps and squeezes. In doing so, she prolonged this state of suspense, schooling herself to wait, sometimes stopping, a finger just hovering over the tip, while the spasms receded.

'Is this right?' Heather gasped, shivering at the wonderful sensations such play produced.

'Make it last. You can learn how. I can keep myself in check – making myself wait for an hour, sometimes, and when I finally come it's cataclysmic.'

Xanthia was finding it nigh impossible to control herself, even as she encouraged Heather to do so. It was too exciting to watch the girl giving a solo performance for the very first time.

Rising, she stood facing Heather, legs apart, feet in the high-heeled sandals, planted firmly on either side. Vainly she sought for a period of grace in which to relish this experience to the full. But the sight of Heather, eyes rolled up, mouth open, one finger moving steadily over her bud, settling into that magical rhythm, was too much.

Xanthia had to let go. 'I can't hold it back any longer!' she moaned, feeling the exquisite sensation of near-orgasm.

Her legs jerked, fingers fluttering over her clitoris, then grinding it harder, till she gave a sharp, light cry, as she reached the limit of endurance, releaving the pressure in one short, savage burst.

Heather was not yet skilled in prolonging the pleasure by waiting. Excited beyond all reckoning by the sight of Xanthia straining in esctasy, she could not stop the movement, coming against her finger, a mighty torrent of pleasure sweeping through her.

It was deep, powerful, one of the most wonderful experiences she had ever known. Like leaping into space and landing safely in her own arms. She cried. The tears ran down her face as she whispered to herself, 'Thank you, thank you.'

Was it selfish? If so, then selfish was good. She had discovered a sense of self that gave her a deep feeling of happiness when she climaxed. Her consciousness expanded. She loved the world and everything in it – wanted to fuck everyone!

She roused at last to find that she was cradled against Xanthia's golden brown breasts, and it was Xanthia's hand that moulded round Heather's sex, as if to protect if from its own violence.

'I'll do it for you soon, and you can caress me,' she murmured, very low. 'But now we'll cuddle up and sleep, shall we? There's another day tomorrow and so many things for you to enjoy. I've yet to introduce you to dildoes and vibrators. Another name for them is Godemiche, such a lovely word. It's latin, you know, and means 'I enjoy myself.' Like the clit, they're designed entirely for female delight.'

Chapter Five

JULIE HAD BEEN one of those privileged to witness the loss of Heather's innocence. She couldn't believe that this beautiful girl had never before known the little death of climax.

'Is it true?' She had kept repeating to André, her juices running, vulva thickening as she watched every move the doctor and his aides made. 'She's really never come? But why? I've been doing it to myself since I was twelve.'

'She was inhibited,' he had replied. 'Her sexuality comatosed, probably through some childhood trauma. And her husband sounds as if he was an insensitive clod.'

His eyes had rested on the television screen to which everything taking place in the consulting room had been transmitted. As he spoke, he had brushed over Julie's nipples lightly, then clapped a hand to her mouth as she had commenced to squeal, saying, 'Shut up! She mustn't know she's being watched.'

After that, Julie's emotions had been on a see-saw – eaten up with jealousy as André thrust his tool into her hand, telling her to rub it, while at the same time he massaged Xanthia's clit. And that magnificent young man whom they called

Jason had opened his fly, produced a ripe member and inserted it in Xanthia's rear.

Why should she be having so much attention? Julie had thought resentfully, her sex throbbing painfully as André responded to the images on the screen and her pressure on his prick, a spurt of hot semen creaming her hand.

When it was over, Xanthia had departed with those who carried Heather back to her room. Julie, left alone with André and Jason, complained bitterly, 'What about me?'

André smiled and gave her an avuncular peck on the cheek. 'What d'you fancy?' he asked.

'You,' she whispered feverishly, clamping her legs round his thigh and rubbing herself against it. 'I love you, André.'

A shutter came down over his eyes and he stepped away from her. 'That's very flattering, but foolish. I want you to learn that it isn't wise to put all your eggs in one basket. I know you've been hurt – you've told me about your years as a battered wife, your broken marriage, the selfish bastards you've been with since. Shatter the mould, Julie. Change direction. Begin with our friend here,' and he clapped Jason round the shoulders. 'Doesn't he appeal to you? Don't you want him to fuck you, or, let's put it another way – don't *you* want to fuck *him*?'

'Will it please you if I do? Will you watch?' She couldn't yet break out of her self-imposed bondage.

Sex meant romantic love to her. Hearts and flowers. Engagement rings. White weddings. Happy ever after. Even though she had suffered a brutal husband who spent all their money on booze and gambling, robbed her of her self-worth and used her as a punch-bag, she still clung to her illusions. Every man she found attractive might be the Mr Right she longed for so much. A steady fellow, a little cottage in the country – babies.

André read her mind, knew the yearnings of her heart, started on his campaign. The Liberation of Julie Foster.

Bidding her wait a while, he went off with Jason. When she was finally called, by the same messenger who had conducted Heather to her baptism of fire, a service lift took her to a room in the basement. By now, under André's instructions, she had changed from masquerade costume into her daily wear of short skirt and neat blouse, the sort of thing she wore to work.

The young county gentleman left her at the door and she walked into the replica of an office. It was all there – chrome fittings, plate-glass, telephone, computer and fax machines – every highly sophisticated adjunct to commerce. Julie prowled round.

There was a shower stall adjacent, and a curtained alcove to one side of it. She discovered that it contained a single bed, plain and severe. There was a rail, too, from which chains, handcuffs, blindfolds, gags and whips dangled. She touched these objects, thrilling at the contrast between cold steel and supple leather.

For whom were these bonds intended? For her? She hoped not and shuddered at the memory of physical pain inflicted on her by men. Turning back into the office she approached the wide desk. On its shining surface stood a card with her name printed in bold script – *Julie Foster, Managing Director*.

Managing Director! *She* was the boss! It didn't much matter what business she was supposed to be involved in. A wide smile lit up her features. My desk. My executive chair. She sank into the glove-leather, swivelled it around, laughing out loud. She had dreamed of one day occupying an important position. This thought amused her for a while. Then she picked up the phone. At once a female voice answered at the other end.

'This is reception. What can I do for you, Miss Foster?'

Glorious moment of power! The excitement of it made Julie grab at her mound through her skirt.

'Have I any more appointments? It's getting late and if we've finished for the day, have the limo sent round to the front entrance,' she pronounced in the tones of an empress.

'There's a client here. He's been waiting for two hours, Miss Foster. Shall I send him down?'

'Yes. Do that. I'll interview him before I go home.'

'Have you forgotten that you're hosting a celebrity ball at the Dorchester this evening?'

'Ah, yes – thank you for reminding me. This won't take long.'

Julie replaced the receiver on its black and ivory cradle and wriggled in the luxurious chair. She felt elated, strong, omnipotent. Just who might this client be?

When he knocked on the door and she called to come in, it was Jason who entered. He had changed jeans and sweat-shirt for brown pin-stripe slacks and a black Giorgio Armani turtleneck. His hair had been groomed and tied back in a pony-tail. He was as drop-dead gorgeous and striking as a Hollywood star about to be photographed by Annie Leibovitz.

That's it. Julie decided. I know who I'm going to be. Oh, wise André! This is indeed a wonderful game. We can ad-lib and make up the rules as we go along.

Jason stood uncertainly just inside the door. 'Take that chair opposite me, where I can look at you more clearly,' Julie said graciously, without rising. But even though she did not appear to move, she was pressing her thighs together under the shelter of the desk, applying pressure to her labia.

'Thank you for seeing me,' he said, seating himself. 'It's most kind. I know you're a very busy lady and have so many demands on your time.'

'That's true, but as a Supermodel agent I'm always prepared to encourage talent. Are you talented?'

'I hope so.' He gave a boyish grin.

'I'm sure you are.' Julie contemplated him, a warm tide of pleasure sweeping through her. She wondered if she could slip a hand between her legs without him noticing, then decided against it. In actual fact, she found herself needing more than the gratification of her own hand.

'Tell me what you've done to date – training – fashion houses and magazines, that kind of thing,' she said crisply and, while he talked, her eyes kept darting to the curtained alcove. She couldn't stop visualising the items there. It was hard to carry on a normal conversation.

Every bit of her skin seemed to have its own particular itch – not of the unpleasant, scratchy kind, but a sort of tickling warmth. Jason's mouth fascinated her. Full, firm lips, strong white teeth. She yearned to feast on him, to suck his prick and take her fill till she was overflowing but never satiated. A diabolical cunning seized her. He wouldn't be allowed to leave her office till she had seduced him.

Restlessness drove her to stand up. He made to rise, too, but her fingers alighted on his shoulders, pressing him down. He would do exactly as she told him. She was so close to him now that she could smell his after-shave, the

82

odour of clean linen, the pungent undertones of shower-gel on masculine genitals.

A shower. That was it. 'I'm due out in a short time and need to wash and change. You can continue talking while I do so. Follow me,' she ordered.

She was already taking off her blouse and reaching behind to unfasten her bra. 'Can I help?' he asked quietly, and his fingers were at the hook, brushing against her skin in lovely intimacy.

She took one look at his dark eyes and the office spun in its axis. Her breasts were bare, the nipples standing proud. She let him gaze at them, but when he reached out a questing hand, brushed it aside, turned on her heel and marched into the shower stall.

It was the matter of seconds to drop her skirt and panties and step under the warm jets. He stood watching her and, all too aware of his eyes, she directed the hose so that it played over her nipples, down across her belly and into her most secret place. It was as if molten lava boiled inside her. The water penetrated her labia which were growing, pulsing, plump and red. Her clitoris jumped, impatient and hungry, desperate for the caress of that humming stream.

She glanced at Jason's slacks. They were of perfect cut, stylish and expensive, but now their shape was distorted by his erection. He dressed to the left, and here the material was stretched over that long, thick shaft which seemed about to burst from the old-fashioned button fastening which had superseded the zip this season.

Denying her impatient bud the satisfaction it was accustomed to obtain on demand, she killed the jet and stepped out of the shower, a white towel looped round her hips.

'What about you?' she asked. 'If you shower,

too, I might let you come to the celebrity party with me. That would do your career a power of good.'

'I want to fuck you,' he said in a husky voice. 'Are you going to let me?'

Julie ran a hand through her wet, tangled hair. 'Not yet,' she answered coolly. 'Maybe never. Take your clothes off and get under the shower.'

Is this really me speaking? she thought in wonder. He wants sexual release and I'm saying no. I've never said no to a man before without feeling guilty. Now I don't feel the smallest twinge of guilt!

Standing naked and open-legged, radiating a kind of sensual aggression, she eyed him as he undressed. Had it been possible for Julie to come without contact with her clitoris, she might have done so in that moment.

He was an Adonis. Wide shoulders tapering to a narrow waist and lean hips, straight thighs, and legs that might have done service as a sculptor's model. His skin was brown all over, as if he sun-bathed nude, and there was a coating of dark hair over his chest. This thinned out to a scrawl tracing across his navel and down into the thick black thatch from which his penis sprang, predatory, massive and ready for action.

Julie leaned over and pushed back the fore-skin. At once his knob emerged further, obscene, slightly ridiculous and deeply fascinating, all at the same time. She wanted to stretch her legs wide and sink down on it till every last inch had been sucked into her body.

'Wash!' she commanded, exerting iron control over her urges.

He obeyed, his prick preceding him into the cubicle. Julie amused herself by likening it to a flag-staff, a sword, a cudgel. And it's mine, all mine, she kept thinking, making sure that he could see her as she fondled her breasts.

When he had finished, she took the towel from him and started to dry him herself. He smelled so good, just like a baby. She wanted to sink her teeth into him, as a mother will her adored infant, not to hurt, just to tease with tiny nibbles and tender love-bites.

Stop it at once! she chided herself. You're not to get soft over him! He's a man. A thing to be used for your pleasure.

He groaned when she dabbed him between the legs and his prick swayed towards her, as if begging for mercy. Julie showed it none, deliberately refusing to touch it. Instead, she grasped his velvety balls, weighing them in her hand, tracing the line between them, then stroking that sensitive area which divided them from his anus. The balls hardened, no longer purple plums but tight, hard chestnuts.

This drove him frantic. He clasped her in his strong arms, rubbed her breasts against his still damp chest, dove a hand down to grip her mound. 'Not yet,' she breathed, though almost as insane with passion herself. 'Kiss me.'

He obeyed, kissing her as she'd never been kissed before. In he went, deep into her throat, and his saliva tasted fresh and sweet. He explored her tongue, every corner of her palate, then withdrew a little to delicately flicker over her lips. Julie wrapped her legs round his thigh, squiggling her hips and rubbing her erect bud backwards and forwards over the muscled length until it was on the point of bursting. She pulled back before this could happen.

The game had only just begun.

'Lie on the couch,' she ordered.

He complied, thinking she was about to allow

penetration. By the time he realised that he had it wrong, it was too late. Alone in her flat, Julie had watched porn movies. There were things done on the screen which she had never encountered, till now. It took her but an instant to fasten the handcuffs round Jason's sinewy wrists, snap them shut and, while he still thought she was joking, attach them to the chains at the head of the bed.

'Hey, what're you doing?' he protested, but laughingly. 'I'm not into SM.'

For answer, she gave his ankles the same treatment. 'Be a good boy, and you won't get hurt,' she advised, her voice thick with excitement.

He lay spread-eagled before her, helpless as a kitten. Julie bit her lip and ruminated on what she might do to him. She eyed the whips, went across and lifted one down, making a few practised swipes through the air. Coming closer to Jason, who was watching her apprehensively, his prick suddenly wilting, she flicked his chest with the tip.

'Ouch!' he exclaimed. 'Don't do that. It stung.'

'Ask me nicely,' she said, leaning over him, one of her breasts just touching his lips. 'Go on. Say it.'

'Say what?' he muttered, his eyes smouldering, even as he raised his head and tried to capture her nipples in his mouth.

'Say – "Please don't hurt me, madam"'

'Please don't hurt me, madam,' he repeated, eyes and mouth sulky.

'That's better.' Julie laid down the whip.

His eyes never left her as she slid a hand over his groin and touched his penis. At once it started to grow and rise, till it was ramrod stiff. Musingly, Julie sat on the side of the couch and played with it, encouraging it to give those odd little leaps that an engorged cock will make, her fist clasped round its base, flipping it from side to side. This was wonderful.

For once, a man was helpless in her hands. She could rouse him to desperation and then leave him tortured with frustration. This had happened to her on numerous occasions when the selfish men in her life had grunted and thrust themselves into orgasm within her, then pulled out, rolled over and gone to sleep. Not this time, she promised herself.

This young god was hers – her toy, her own personal play-thing. He would do precisely what she wanted or he'd get a taste of the whip. She hoped he wasn't one of those people who enjoyed being beaten, for it was not her intention to add to his pleasure by the kiss of the lash.

With consummate skill, she worked his cock, rubbing it till he begged for release, then holding off. After a moment, she sat astride his thighs and, taking hold of it again, started to lick it, using the same long tongued motion as if she was eating ice-cream. A chocolate-coated bar, she decided, her tongue running up it from base to tip, in slow, lingering strokes. Then she circled the glans, stretching the foreskin back as far as it would go. She could see glistening drops forming on its head, that pre-ejaculation juice tasted so good. Julie sipped it, then removed her lips.

'For Christ's sake!' Jason groaned, strung out in a fearsome agony of pleasure.

Julie smiled. Sitting back, her knees raised and a leg on either side of the prone man, she lifted her breasts in both hands, caressing the nipples. By now she was crazy for orgasm, but enjoyed the protracted love-play as never before. Leaving her receptive breasts, she placed a hand each side of her labia, holding back the slick-wet folds. Her clitoris was swollen, a homologue of the penis, but far superior. By comparison, a man's organ was a dull, blunt instrument.

She slithered up his body, feeling his skin pressed against her anus and slippery cleft, up and up till she was sitting on his chest, his gaze in direct line with her sex. Still keeping the pink area held open with two fingers of her left hand, she used the middle finger of the right, her favourite means of self-gratification, to gently rub her clit. To have him so close, watching her, was deliriously exciting. Up and down her finger went, sometimes circling the tender tip, petting it, subjecting it to a short burst of frenzied rubbing, then returning to that delicious wet stroking.

She schooled herself to wait. 'I want you to suck it,' she said. 'Ask me nicely if you can do it.'

'I want to! Oh, yes – let me,' he pleaded, his face beaded with sweat.

Now Julie kneeled over his face, dipping down so that he could lick her juices and take that hard button between his lips. He tongued it, nibbled it, sucked it into his mouth. The feeling gathered uncontrollably as his tongue worked faster, and, flinging back her head, breasts held in her hands as she mimicked the strokes on her nipples, Julie came in an explosive spasm of intense pleasure.

She collapsed on him like a felled animal, then, while the ripples were still undulating through her, impaled herself on his needy weapon. Her inner muscles clenched round it and, hips gyrating, she ground herself down on it, devouring every last inch. He was panting, groaning, thrusting up into her, his semen pumping from his testicles to burst out in a great torrent inside her.

Heather woke with bright sunlight shining in her eyes. She was instantly alert, feeling absolutely normal and just plain hungry. No hangover, which was surprising considering that she had felt quite drunk last night.

Shrugging her shoulders into her satin dressing-gown (old habits die hard and she still couldn't accept the fact that it was perfectly correct to pad about her room mother-naked) she went out on to the balcony.

There were pale wisps of mist clinging to the tree-tops, vapourising even as she watched, a brilliance over all that promised another hot day. The garden sparkled below her – green lawns and colourful flower-beds – a terrace, and the glimmer of a swimming pool that looked like a fallen patch of sky.

The view seemed extra bright, as if scales had been removed from her eyes, and she aware of everything much more clearly than before. Sight, hearing, taste, touch – all had been enhanced by her experiences of last night.

There were loungers ringing the pool, and the bronzed figure reclining on one of them raised her arm and waved.

'Come on down,' Xanthia carolled. 'It's a glorious morning. Breakfast is being served out here.'

Heather couldn't see anyone else about. She wondered where Xanthia's other guests were. Had they also been given the treatment during the dark hours?

She rummaged in the drawer of the Sheraton tallboy in which she had stashed her underwear, finding her black swimming costume, a sleek, backless number, the high cut of the sides making her legs seemed incredibly long. After showering, she wriggled into it, smoothing the stretchy material over her body. Stuffing a bottle of coconut oil in a hold-all, along with a paperback for she hoped to be able to catch up on her reading, she draped a large beach-towel over her shoulders, adjusted her sun-glasses and found her way downstairs.

There a footman directed her to the conservatory, a jungly place with a humid atmosphere, green ironwork funiture of Victorian vintage, and freakish vegetation that resembled triffids. French doors gave access to the terrace.

Heather was nervous of meeting her hostess in the cold light of day. When she had closed her eyes and slept, Xanthia had been there – warm naked arms embracing her, slender fingers stroking over her hair. It was impossible to know when she had departed, but it looked as if she had been in the garden for some time.

The strong bouquet of Turkish coffee stimulated Heather's nostrils as she walked, barefoot, over ochre-hued terrazzo tiles. They were already warm, and she imagined that they'd become unbearably hot by noon. The patio was laid out in Spanish style, the balmy Cornish air kind to the semi-tropical plants tumbling over the edges of stone tubs and sprawled from hanging baskets in a riot of colour.

Heather adored Spain, and owned a villa there, so she felt more at home as she walked across to where Xanthia lay by the pool's rim. She wore nothing but a G-string, a tiny triangle of leopard-spotted fabric that just covered her mount of venus. There wasn't a trace of pubic hair visible, though there should have been, the strip of cloth being so narrow.

Xanthia, propped on one elbow on the

cushioned pad of the lounger, correctly inter-
preted her glance, laughed and said, 'I use an
Egyptian wax, a secret formula employed in the
harems. Sultans like their concubines to be
hairless. I only do the bikini line, my dear. Rather
fond of the sight of my lips sprouting from my
little nest. But a thong looks more attractive
without fronds sticking out at the sides. Would
you like me to apply some to you?'

Heather blushed, still uneasy with Xanthia's
frank way of talking, even though they had
watched each other masturbate last night. 'No,
thanks,' she replied, taking a vacant lounger. 'I
don't wear bikinis.'

'You should – or nothing, preferably. There are
few things more unsightly than strap marks. One
needs to be tanned all over, or not bother.'
Xanthia always expressed her opinions forcibly. It
was nigh impossible to argue with her. 'I never sit
in the sun unless I can take everything off.'

'Well, I still like the one-piece,' Heather said
meekly. 'In any case, I don't have anything else.'

'No problem,' Xanthia replied, then fished in
her canvas tote bag and held out a package, still in
its plastic wrapper that carried a Harrods label.
'Here. Try this. I haven't worn it yet.'

Oh, dear – no excuse now, Heather thought,
glancing around her. 'I'll take it indoors and pop
it on, shall I?'

'No need,' Xanthia declared, and her green
eyes considered Heather's slim body with the
hungry look usually associated with a lecherous
male. 'We're the only ones about yet, apart from
the servants and one doesn't count them. I'm
dying to see you naked again, my precious
darling. You're so beautiful.'

I can't refuse her, Heather concluded, and
slipped down the shoulder-straps of her costume.

Here goes! In for a penny, in for a pound, I suppose.

The sun struck like flaming arrows on her bare skin, especially those areas unaccustomed to exposure. On a sudden surge of defiance (against what? Against whom? Her mother, perhaps – the nuns at the convent school she had attended?) Heather rolled down the rest of the swimsuit and kicked it aside.

'Bravo!' Xanthia cried.

'Encore!' said a masculine voice, and André strolled across the terrace, clapping his hands together.

Too late to hide now. Face averted, Heather took the tiny triangle out of its cellophane envelope and slipped it over her pubis, the long thong attached to it disappearing up the crease between her buttocks. From there it emerged on either side to join the thin straps that rose over her hip bones.

Its pressure on her secret parts made her shiver. This increased when, on glancing down, she saw her fuzz poking out. It didn't look right, and she knew that Xanthia had been correct. It would be better to be entirely naked. That, at least, had some dignity about it.

She shot an envious glance across to where her hostess lay in all her glory – golden brown skin glistening with oil, narrow strip of dark plastic across her eyes, her hair pinned high, a few tendrils curling over her ears. She moved like a svelte tigress, untieing the tanga, rolling over so that her slender, shapely back was in full view – boyish rump, long brown thighs. Propped up on her elbows, she never took her eyes from Heather.

'I will have to do something about your pubic hair,' she commented lazily, while André leaned over and brushed his lips across her cheek, then went to the rattan table and poured himself a *demi-tasse*.

'Take if off, meantime,' he suggested, giving his charming, quirky grin as he stared at Heather from behind his dark glasses, sipping the savoury brew. Then, realising that she didn't have a cup, asked, 'Cream and sugar, or do you like it black?'

'Cream, please. No sugar.' Heather untied the thong and removed it, thinking, how odd to be conversing as naturally as if they were at a vicarage coffee-morning. She's naked, so am I, and he's obviously becoming aroused by the sight.

He came across with a cup for her, wearing a pair of baggy cotton shorts in a jazzy pattern, but even the fullness could not disguise his tumescent penis. He, too, was bronzed, a well-muscled man who kept his body in trim. Heather sat down hurriedly on a spare lounger. It was deep and she sank into its padded surface. This way her bottom and mound were hidden. She was becoming quite blasé about the bareness of her breasts.

'Protective oil!' Xanthia said. 'Never sit in the sun without it. André, will you do the honours?' And she reached beneath her couch and handed him a gold and orange bottle containing an expensive product.

'With pleasure,' he grinned, his shadow blotting out the sun momentarily as he stood in front of Heather.

She wanted to say that it was all right – she'd manage herself, but the sight of the handsome man carefully pouring a little puddle of aromatic oil into his cupped palm made her heart jump and her bud throb. Silently, she put down her coffee-cup and stretched out on her back.

André began with her feet, his hands gentle as a woman's as he worked the oil over the toes, the slender ankles, and moved up the shins. Heather lay with an arm over her eyes as if to shield them from the sun's glare, even though her face was shadowed by a large raffia parasol. In reality, she wanted to concentrate on the lovely sensations his hands were producing in her newly aware cleft.

They caressed her knees and began their slow progress up her thighs. Heather's legs parted involuntarily and she raised her pubis wantonly, offering herself to his touch. But his hands slid away, skirting her mound and skimming over her belly, past the narrow waist, the taut ribcage, the full curves of her breasts.

She lifted them as he made circular sweeps of each one, grazing the nipples, smoothing the oil into them. 'This is a most tender area,' he commented, on his hunkers beside her. 'It would be painful if they became sun-burnt, wouldn't it?'

Heather opened her eyes, head to one side. André's body was so angled that she could see up the left leg of his shorts. She looked straight into the single eye of his engorged penis. It was a shock – sending tremors through her, accentuating the torment and delight of his touch. She was disappointed when he moved and the view changed abruptly.

He massaged the oil into her shoulders and neck, then, 'That's it, darling,' he said, rising to his feet. 'In half an hour I'll do your back. And you must give your sides attention, too. Xanthia will time you.'

Heather was burning, waves of feeling travelling all the way through her spine down to the base. She had the crazy impulse to grab André's hand and place it where she needed it most. By his expression, she knew that he was aware.

'And where, André, is the inestimable Julie?' Xanthia asked, half sitting up, watching them avidly, her tongue moistening her red lips.

He laughed. 'Last seen dressed entirely in black leather, high-heeled boots, open-crotched panties, open-tipped bra – the whole bit, leading one of our more, shall we say, innovative, male guests round the grounds. He was wearing a dog collar – naked, chained, on his hands and knees. He was loving every minute of it. So was she.'

'Ah, so she's no longer a doormat and has discovered her forte as a dominatrix?' Xanthia's stared at him, her eyes narrowed against the dazzling light.

'It certainly looks that way.' He bent over and smoothed the surplus oil from his hands over her belly and crease. 'She was using a whip, but permitting her 'doggie' to lick her through the slash in her panties. I think I may have lost my servile secretary.'

'Don't worry, I'll employ her here, if she's that good.'

André allowed his lips to follow the path of his fingers, and Xanthia heaved against his mouth, coming almost instantaneously. He patted her pubis affectionately, licked her juices from his lips with obvious relish, and turned to Heather once more.

'Shall we swim? Don't worry about the oil, it's water-repellent,' he said, and going to the edge of the pool, divested himself of his shorts. His cock shot forth, large, with prominent veins running up the trunk, the glans shining.

'Yes, I'd like that.' Heather welcomed the idea of coolness quenching the fire blazing in her loins. To swim nude would be a novel experience.

'Are you coming in?' André addressed Xanthia who, resting from one orgasm and looking

95

forward to the next, was basking in the hot sunshine like a Mediterranean lizard.

'In a minute.' She picked up her mobile phone and spoke into it. 'Oh, Jean, could you locate Paul and ask him if he's free? I'm on the south terrace. OK?'

Heather waded into the pool by way of the wide tiled steps that curved along one end. The water was azure blue, reflecting the colour of the mosaics with which it was lined. André, meanwhile, dived into the deep end, rising to the surface quickly, throwing the dripping hair back from his eyes.

The water was delicious, silky and warm as Heather struck out, swimming strongly. She had always been at home in this element, sometimes wishing that she had been born a sea-creature, a dolphin, perhaps, who played in the ocean all day, chirruping and clicking as it communicated with its fellows. How simple, harmonious and uncomplicated such an existence would be.

The water rippled across her naked flesh, and she delighted in the sensation of its touch on the private places of her body. André was close to her now. She felt his fingers on her breasts, but darted away, unwilling to let anything interrupt her watery delight.

At last, she rested against the rim, her feet on the tiled flooring, wavelets lapping her nipples. He leaned on his elbows beside her, showering her with sparkling drops. It was then that she became aware of another presence. A young man was stalking across the terrace towards Xanthia.

He wore a loose-fitting white suit and shirt, and this contrasted almost shockingly with his dark skin. He was perhaps the most perfect example of an Afro-Caribbean male that Heather had ever seen – lithe, superbly graceful, long legged and loose hipped. He moved with the regality of a chieftain – gold glinting about his person, at his wrists, around his throat, on those long, aristocratic-looking fingers. His black dreadlocks flowed over his shoulder and halfway down his back.

'Paul, darling,' she heard Xanthia say in that rich, seductive voice of hers. 'Won't you join us?'

'Anything for you, babe,' he answered amiably, leaning over to give her a casual greeting kiss.

Xanthia rose. She was superb, a sex goddess, globular breasts with spiky, oiled nipples, the thin line of hair remaining on her mound revealing the high, sharply defined cleft. She took Paul by the hand, her skin almost as deeply coloured as his, and led him to the pool where they stood gazing down.

'Paul, this is Heather,' she said, smiling wickedly. 'Our new pupil, who is proving most apt at her lessons.'

'Hi, Heather,' he said, and gave her a slow smile that rendered his face even more beautiful.

'Hello,' she said faintly, riveted by this vision in front of her.

His eyes were like golden brown agates, the lashes impossibly long and curling. His flesh ran like coffee-cream over his high, flat cheekbones, and his mouth was the red of the hibiscus blossom, while his teeth matched the whites of his eyes. Handsome and proud, he aimed his beauty like an arrow at her heart, or rather straight at her loins which quivered in response.

Xanthia was impatient. She couldn't keep her hands off Paul, helping him undress, lingering on the area between his legs. Naked, he was even more stunning. Muscular without being over-developed, his body rippled under that gleaming dark skin, and his shaft rose from the ebony

97

thatch between his thighs. It was bigger than André's, long and thick, the bare head purplish in hue.

Before Heather realised what was happening, the four of them were in the water together, and then she felt hands all over her, on her breasts, pulling at her nipples, opening her sex, a frisson of excitement scalding along her nerves. Xanthia and Paul supported her in the water. She felt light as a feather as they spread her legs and lowered her on to André's prick. With their aid, she moved up and down, feeling it expand inside her, missing the sensation of a finger on her clitoris – a cock wasn't enough. It might fill her, excite her with its size chafing against the inner ridges of her vagina, but it would fail to give her an orgasm.

She wriggled and strained against him, tormented by Xanthia's fingers rousing her nipples. Then André stopped fucking her, withdrawing with his ejaculation still intact. Heather floated into Paul's arms, her face buried in his wet locks. He smelled of spices and heat, salty skin against her lips, then his mouth, his tongue pushing between her teeth, even as his penis pressed urgently against her belly.

Up she was raised in his strong black arms, and then gently lowered on to his enormous prick. In order to allow him greater penetration, she clamped her legs about his waist, while the water sloshed around them and she could hear Xanthia's animal cries as André penetrated and pleasured her. Heather wound her arms round Paul's neck, rising and falling, slipping and sliding on that gigantic organ.

He gasped, groaned, opened his gleaming brown eyes and smiled at her. 'D'you like this, or shall we go somewhere else? Your place, or mine?'

She nodded, clung to him, grateful for his

understanding, and he carried her effortlessly up the steps out of the pool, and across the terrace, snatching up a towel on the way.

Finding a nook on the grass behind some bushes, he laid her down, stretched out beside her, and proceeded to caress her breasts, kiss and stroke her swelling bud till she cried out with the force of the powerful climax that shuddered through her.

Then, and only then, did Paul mount her, pumping hard into her still convulsing vagina until he, too, came in a pounding flood of feeling that drew a trimuphant yell from his lips.

Chapter Six

WITHOUT BOTHERING TO do more than wrap sarongs around their loins, they ate lunch in a shady corner of the patio. It was all very relaxed and casual, no formal settings, no other people present.

'This is my private playground,' Xanthia explained. 'There are more terraces and a further pool which my other visitors can use. You're special, Heather,' and she added with an impish grin. 'Did you enjoy your swim?'

Heather nodded, still thrilling from the screw with Paul. He was seated further away, absorbed in a game of chess with André. On the stone table was a wealth of cold chicken, smoked salmon and salad, the tomatoes bigger, redder, juicier, the lettuce and endives lusciously green, and fresher than any Heather had seen before. Certainly no one could complain about the cuisine at Tostavyn Grange.

'I like Paul,' she said, settling back with a full plate on her lap. 'He's gentle.'

'And hung like a stallion,' Xanthia proclaimed, sucking small pale grapes into her mouth, relishing the crisp, satisfying pop that released the hidden liquid. 'Gentle? You like that?'

'Of course. Doesn't every woman?' Heather

asked, puzzled. 'He was careful to satisfy me, spent ages rubbing the head of his penis against my clitoris, then moving it up and down until I came. Only then did he stick his dick in me. It felt so good, and seemed to go on pumping for ever.'

Xanthia, looking thoughtful, was filling two crystal goblets with sparkling white wine. Then she sat back, the sarong falling open over her thighs, dislaying the shadowy area of her groin. 'Oh, yes – gentleness is fine, but one needs a contrast. Cruder handling, perhaps? Haven't you heard that ladies sometimes like "a bit of rough"?'

Heather's arched brows drew down in a worried little frown. 'That's a horrible idea. Are you suggesting rape? Surely not. It's a terrible crime against a woman – a cruel invasion of her body, mind and soul. Unforgivable!'

'Darling, calm down.' Xanthia leaned over and ran a caressing hand over Heather's hair, then trailed it down her neck and over her breasts, lingering on the nipples. 'Of course the reality is appalling, but we're not talking real life in any of the scenes you'll play while you're here. I remember a line I read in a novel somewhere once. It went like this: "She waited breathlessly, wanting him to take her willingly – by force." D'you get my drift? I've something interesting planned for you later.'

No matter how Heather pleaded, Xanthia merely smiled mysteriously and told her to wait and see. The afternoon drifted by on golden, idle wings. Music filled the air – sensual, dreamy. Heather drank deeply of the delicious cocktail Xanthia prepared, and felt so totally limp and receptive that she suspected there was something more than alcohol in the brew. She wouldn't put it past Xanthia to use aphrodisiacs.

Then, when the sun was starting to dip behind

101

the trees, casting long mauve shadows across the pool, Xanthia got up, stretched her glorious naked limbs, and accompanied Heather to her room.

'Change into this,' she ordered, pointing to a costume spread out on the bed.

'What is it?' Heather picked up the gown. It was made of bottle-green wool so fine as to be almost transparent. From her knowledge of period costumes, the cut and style was vaguely medieval, though could have been much earlier.

'You're a Saxon princess,' Xanthia said. 'Time, the Dark Ages – around 800 AD.' She added with a grin, 'No panties. Respectable women never wore drawers. They were thought most immodest garments, associated with breeches worn by men. If a husband found out that his wife had knickers on, then he was convinced she was being unfaithful. Just shows you how stupid men are and always have been. Here, let me help you dress.'

The gown was perfect, the bodice fitting tightly over Heather's breasts, and fastened with thongs from the pit of her throat to just below the waist. The skirt flowed over her hips and flared out at the hem. The sleeves were long, and tight at the wrists. A heavy torque of Celtic design composed of swirls carved into the bronze was clasped around her neck. This was her only ornament, save for a plain gold fillet which Xanthia placed low across her brow. Her hair was down, a shining sepia waterfall cascading over the shoulders of the serge, fur-trimmed mantle.

Xanthia stood, head on one side, admiring her handiwork. 'Fine. You'll do.'

'Are there no shoes?' It gave Heather a start to see herself reflected in the cheval-mirror. My God, she thought, is this really me?'

102

She was handed a pair of leather half-boots, and the transormation was complete. Heather drew herself up proudly, ribs lifted, nipples pointing heavenwards, chin tilted at a haughty angle.

'You look every inch a king's daughter,' Xanthia commented, green eyes dancing. 'Have you ever thought seriously of taking up acting as a career?'

'Maybe,' Heather said, unable to resist adopting the regal manner befitting a princess. 'And what is tonight's scenario?'

'You don't need to know much. Suffice to say that you're Princess Morgana, and that you've been entrusted to take an important message from your royal father to one of his military commanders. Just play it by ear. You'll carry it off – when the time comes.' Xanthia was bubbling with excitement.

As she visualisd the sequence she had arranged, so a thrill shot along her nerves, making her nipples prick and rousing that peeping sentinel ever alert as it stood on guard at the top of her cleft. What a marvellous occupation she had! Giving pleasure – taking it herself.

She guided Heather down the stairs, through the garden to where the surrounding forest began. It was gloomy there, and Heather felt the first twinge of apprehension, though, far from frightening her, it sent the adrenaline coursing through her veins.

Xanthia opened the arched gate and gave her a little shove. Heather found herself outside. It closed smartly and she was alone. There was no turning back.

Silence came down like a pall. The tops of the trees flamed in the setting sun, the sky eggshell blue streaked with orange in the west, the rest plunged into darkness. An uneven, stony path beckoned, a pale, sandy streak winding downwards through the crowding foliage. Heather, head held high, stiffened her spine and started to walk.

Every creak of a branch or rustle of a leaf made her jump, hand flying to the jewelled hilt of the small dagger she wore in her belt. She felt that she was in terrible danger if she fell into the wrong hands, whose she wasn't yet sure.

The trees and shrubs thinned. Salt spiced the air, and there was the thunder of great crested Cornish waves crashing against the cliffs. Now the descent was more difficult, the path forming into rough-hewn steps. Heather proceded cautiously, so intent on keeping her footing that it wasn't until she had reached the beach and rounded a jutting pile of rocks that she became aware of a light other than that of the sinking sun, a flaming ball on the horizon.

Then, and by this time it was too late to retreat, she saw that it came from a huge bonfire. Flames thundered up towards the night clouds rushing in and, in that lurid glow, she was able to discern a crowd of outlandish figures. In the next second vicelike arms locked about her body.

She thrashed and kicked, but the man who held her grinned evilly, dragging her into the circle of crimson light. Now she could see the serpent prow of the long-boat anchored in the shallows of the cove – now, heart leaping into her mouth, she recognised her captors. The shaggy hides, the thonged trousers, the helmets. They were bearded, their hair long or plaited, bristling with weapons – axes – broad-swords.

She had been captured by her father's deadly enemies – those blood-thirsty and ruthless Norseman who terrorised the coast, leaving behind a swathe of death, pillage and rape whenever one of their dragon-headed ships crept up the shore.

'Let me go!' Heather shouted, ragingly indignant, yet wondering which one had been detailed to ravish her. Clever Xanthia! How could she have known that Vikings had always fascinated Heather? She inwardly applauded her hostess.

The raiders roared with laughter, throwing her from one to the other, their hands squeezing her breasts, pushing up her skirts. Then a man stepped out of the gloom, his presence such that his unruly followers abruptly let her go.

He was a stunning sight in the fire-shot twilight. Immensely tall, his scarlet cape emphasising his broad shoulders. The head of a wolf which he wore, its pelt flowing down his back, was in direct contrast to the flaxen hair that merged with it. Magnificent, barbaric, her first glimpse of him made a coil of longing clench in Heather's womb, while her clitoris throbbed demandingly.

'What's all this?' His deep voice echoed among the sombre cliffs, rising abover the clamour of the sea.

'A prisoner, my Lord Ragnar!' one of his men declaimed, the very ruffian who had discovered Heather.

'Well done, Olaf. You've captured a rare bird indeed.'

Ragnar paced slowly towards her, not stopping until he stood but a single step away, looming over her. The saltiness of the sea reached her nostrils more powerfully, emanating from him – combined with leather, the feral odour of the wolf-hide – the musky, heady sweat of the man himself.

Remember your role as a proud princess, she

reminded herself. Don't fling yourself into his arms and grab at his cock as every instinct is urging you to do!

'How dare your beasts treat me so roughly!' she shouted, glaring up defiantly into his fierce blue eyes set in that hard, bearded face.

He threw back his head and laughed, hands on his hips, legs astraddle. 'You're my prisoner, wench!' he retorted. 'I'll do with you as I will.'

Then, swift as a striking snake, one of the massive tanned hands shot out and gripped the neck of her gown. In one swift jerk, he ripped it to the waist. She made to fling up her arms to cover her bare breasts, but Olaf, standing behind her, seized her wrists and spread them wide, displaying her beauty for all to see.

The men closed in, leering at her, but she was aware only of the expression on Ragnar's craggily handsome features as he ran his eyes over her. That look, her own excitement, the chill air, caused her nipples to form into red-brown peaks.

She was helpless as his big hands cupped each globe, calloused thumbs rubbing across the nipples. Heather could feel herself melting – knees, thighs – her vulva expelling those juices which would make for his easy entry.

'Unhand me!' she hissed, her eyes murderous. 'My father will have you flayed alive for this insult. I'm Princess Morgana!'

'Ah, but your father isn't here, Princess. Indeed we vanquished him in battle but an hour since. There's no one to aid you.' Ragnar's voice was mocking, his hands tightening on her resisting body. 'I must show the men a good example. It pleases me to prepare a captive woman for my mercenaries.'

He swooped, and swung her over one wide, mail-clad shoulder. She found herself hanging, head down, hair streaming, beating with her fists against his uncaring back, while his men cheered and shouted.

'Put me down, you bastard!' she shrieked.

Ignoring her, he strode towards his tent, a crude construction of hides. The flap fell back into place behind them and she was alone with him in the darkness relieved only by a rushlight. With a jolt that shocked right through her, Ragnar dumped her down on the heap of furs that served as his bed.

She lay back on her elbows, glaring up at him. How tall he was, how powerful. How strong those arms that had clamped under her buttocks and at her back as he carried her. The set-up was so realistic that she could almost believe she was a captive princess at the mercy of her conqueror. She experienced the fear, could smell the rutting heat of his body, and taste her own raging desire on her tongue.

Never taking his eyes from her, Ragnar threw of his cloak, mail, girdle, then his tunic, and unbound the thongs before removing his leather leggings.

Heather's breath rasped in her throat, the ache in her groin rising to become a serious pain as she looked at his warrior's body. Her tongue came out to lick her lower lip, the throbbing in her heart increasing in tempo, matching that of the pulsing in her sex.

Ragnar's wide chest glinted with golden hair, a long crooked scar of some old wound slashed across it. She wanted to run her fingers down it, then tongue the nipples that stood out taut on the firm muscles. Thick sinewy legs supported him like solid pillars and, springing from the tangled hair that furred his lower belly, his shaft – like an iron rod – pointing at Heather imperiously, selecting her as the receptacle for its outpouring of seed.

She shook her head slowly. 'Oh, no! You can't – the gods will wreak vengeance on you if you touch me. I'm holy. Don't you understand?'

His brow shot up, a smile curling his wide mouth. 'A virgin?'

Now do I say yes or no? Heather consulted the script-writers in her brain. I've got to be a virgin, surely? A king's daughter, as yet unwedded, maidenhead intact.

'You insult me, savage!' she hissed. 'Of course I'm a virgin.'

His smile deepened. 'Good,' he said. 'I'll make you my wife, Morgana, and the bride of Ragnar the Sea-wolf must be chaste. I'll take no other man's leavings.'

'Your wife?' The contempt in her voice cut like a lash. 'You think I'd marry *you* – a Viking – the scum of the ocean?'

His face darkened with anger, amazingly blue eyes flashing with rage. 'I, too, am a king. I can enjoy and leave you, or honour you with marriage.'

He lunged at her but she danced out of his reach, snatching her dagger from its sheath. 'You ruffian!' she screamed. 'I could stab you to death without remorse. Beware! If you lay a finger on me again, I'll kill you and then turn the knife on myself!'

'Vixen!' he growled. 'Put that down before you cut yourself.'

'Damn you!'' she cried and flung herself on him, catching him off balance. Her arm swung back and the knife flashed in a downward arc.

'Bitch!' he grated, and closed in on her, grabbing the wrist that held the blade, yanking her arm behind her.

Heather responded by struggling frantically, trying to knee him in the groin – not too seriously though, she did not wish to damage him there!

Their thrashing limbs knocked against a rough-hewn bench and sent it flying. The rush-light guttered, wooden mugs and platters scattering in all directions. Heather, all too aware of his rampant staff pressing into her as they fought, could make little impression on his steely muscles. His grip tightened brutally on her wrists. The pain became unendurable and her fingers slowly opened. The knife dropped to the sand.

It was over. He pushed her down on the furs and threw himself beside her. Though she twisted her head from side to side, he possessed her lips. She was dazed and dizzy, throbbing with desire. He deepened his kiss, penetrating the honeyed sweetness of her mouth as he would soon penetrate her body. He darted his tongue between her lips repeatedly, using the motions of sex, as if it was a second cock.

His hands went to her breasts, stroking them firmly, dallying over the hungry peaks, then rolling them between his fingers. His beard grazed her cheek, and even that increased the trembling she couldn't control. His cock pressed against her belly, urgent and hard. The force of it, so brutal, so animal in its primitive need, made her suck her breath through her teeth. She wanted to have him plunder the depths of her, to press into her womb, hurting her with its size.

Never before had she been so conscious of the sheer power of a man, or been more acutely aware of her own physical weakness. What was he going to do? Hurt her? Torture her? She gasped as shivers seized her. Her lips were dry, her sex wet.

'Don't tremble so, Princess,' he whispered, very low, his breath tickling her ear.

'Please let me go,' she begged, pressing her hands against the golden breadth of his chest. 'You'll be amply rewarded.'

'Ah, child, you still don't understand, do you?' There was a note of regret in his voice, and his hands gentled her like a nervous filly. 'You no longer have a kingdom. It's gone. Destroyed.'

'By you, bastard!' she cried, squirming under him. 'I'd rather die than be your wife.'

Anger blazed in his eyes. He stopped caressing her, rearing above her, forcing open her thighs with one knee and ramming his tool into her. Heather cried out, unprepared for such a sudden assault, yet something dangerous and primitive deep within her responded to this man's selfish, one-pointed pursuit of orgasm.

There was his engorged cock: there was a hole into which he must plunge it. He was blind to everything except the overwhelming need to sate himself. He no longer cared who lay beneath him. She could have been a toothless hag but, once he had a hard-on, he would still have been driven by that primordial urge.

Heather understood his impatience, surrendering to its unconditional violence, experiencing a perverse satisfaction in the fact that her conqueror was concerned solely with his own pleasure, without bothering about hers. Yet it was frustrating; bruised, burning with desire, Heather tried to position herself so that his frantic penis rubbed against her clit, but it was impossible. Her movements only succeded in accelerating the speed of his fucking and, in one last frenzied burst of energy, he spent himself within her.

He lay across her, half smothering her with his bulk. Realising that he had finished, she was consumed with fury. 'Get off, barbarian!' she snarled.

He muttered and rolled over then, to her extreme annoyance, shifted away from her, exactly as Charles had done on their wedding night. In a second he was deeply asleep.

'Inconsiderate sod!' Heather muttered. 'Jesus Christ, if this is what the Vikings did then I can understand why women hated being ravished by them.'

She got up, aware of his still warm emission trickling down her inner thighs. She grabbed up his tunic and dried herself on it, then flung it down across his face with a gesture of supreme contempt. Just for a moment, she stood there staring at that magnificent body which had proved, after all, to be such a disappointment. She picked up her mantle and shrugged it over her shoulders, then ran the thumb over the dagger's sharp edge. If she had really been Princess Morgana, no doubt she would have plunged it into his heart before making her escape.

But she was Heather Logan, civilised twentieth-century woman, who could not kill an unsatisfactory lover, much as she would have enjoyed doing so.

She lifted the tent flap. The camp was dead quiet, the men sleeping by the fire, wrapped in their cloaks. Moving with the speed and silence of a wraith, Heather went back the way she had come, finding that someone, doubtless at Xanthia's behest, had stuck flares into the rocks and through the woods to light her path back to the house.

The first thing Heather did on reaching her room was to run a hot bath. Her mind was buzzing and sleep out of the question. Paramount was the need to see Xanthia and talk over this latest

111

episode. She had discovered that a good deal of her enjoyment of these sexual encounters came from discussing them afterwards with that experienced, worldly woman.

Lying in the soothing, perfumed water, she let her fingers idle over her breasts, soaping the nipples so that they stood rosily among the snowy suds. Down went her hand, across her belly, shampooing her pubic hair, making little foamy swirls in the crisp dark bush. She opened her legs. Warm water laved her labia. The pink wings opened at the touch of her finger – clean, shiny, her bud beginning to rise from its hood.

She stroked it. It prickled. A vision of Ragnar's huge cock flashed behind her closed eyelids. Her sex ached. Teasing her clit, she left it, concentrating on her nipples. Two at once gave her delicious sensations. She wished she had three hands, for her clit needed rubbing, too. By squeezing her breasts together and holding them there with her arms stiff, she was able to reach both nipples with one hand. This left the other free to dive down into the water and land on that little nub which was frantic for contact.

So busy was she that she didn't realise she was no longer alone till Xanthia said, 'Ah, so Ragnar did not satisfy you?'

Heather, caught out while masturbating, stopped at once, her cheeks flaming. She sat up in the water and got busy with the sponge and soap. 'No, he didn't. How did you know that?'

'I guessed.' Xanthia sat on the edge of the tub. 'The men who make the most noise about it are generally the lousiest lovers.'

'A pity, for he has a superb body.'

'I know. Such a waste,' Xanthia agreed, then added, 'but you found the whole thing fun?'

'I did. The element of fear is most stimulating.

But, oh, Xanthia, I do so want to come!' Heather couldn't pretend any longer, her need was too great. 'I almost wish you hadn't shown me how. Now I'm constantly aware of my clit. It wants attention all the time.'

'I'm glad.' Xanthia dipped a hand into the bath-water. It homed in on Heather's cleft, gently probing the bud that became instantly alert. 'But you must learn to wait, thus extending the pleasure. I've kept it going for hours sometimes, refusing to allow myself to climax. And then, when the stress becomes too great and I finally give in, it's a tremendous spasm of exquisite sensation, wave after wave of it – I tingle from my toes to my scalp.'

As she spoke of this, Xanthia was getting excited. Her free hand caressed herself through the thin fabric of the gown she wore. This was a simple robe consisting of two halves that covered her body front and back, held in at the waist with a silken gridle. But, being open at both sides, every time she moved it was to show a dazzling glimpse of bare breasts or a long sweep of thigh.

Her friend's action of fingering her own labia caused Heather to tremble with need. Xanthia smiled that deep, knowing smile and said, 'Time to go. On with the next phase.'

'Can't I come first?' Heather pleaded.

'No.' Xanthia was adamant. 'I want you out of the bath and raring to go.'

Heather sighed, gave her mound a small consolatory pat, and rose, dripping, from the tub. 'What d'you want me to wear this time?' she asked rather sulkily, thinking, really I'm getting very selfish about sex. Like a child denied its lollypop.

Xanthia was standing in the bedroom, the light from the bedside lamp outlining her limbs through her diaphanous robe. She pressed one finger against her temples, as if considering the problem. 'Not too much,' she said at last. 'But something tantalising. We're about to help Julie with her disciplinary measures. Some of the gentlemen positively revel in this. It's our job to give them what they want.'

She flung open the armoire and took out some garments which might have graced a store catering for heavy bikers. 'Let's dress as a couple of Hell's Angels' 'old ladies'. That will be amusing. Leather is always a turn-on.'

Heather felt slightly ridiculous after dressing. She wore a minute black calfskin skirt which just covered her mound. Suspenders ran down her thighs, before and aft, meeting the tops of fishnet stockings. High boots encased her legs, the stack heels making walking difficult. Her bodice was extremely tight and brief, her breasts bulging at the deep opening, held together by laces at the front.

Xantha grinned widely, posing in a tiny leather bra and skin-tight trousers with an open crotch. She had buckled wide studded straps round her wrists, and teased out her hair into a cloudy mass framing her painted face – she looked like the sort of tart that hung around bikers' cafés – ready, eager and willing for a gang-bang.

Before they went down into the basement, Xanthia gave Heather another of those spiked drinks, so that by the time they reached Julie's 'office', she was feeling high as a kite.

'Come in,' Julie called. She sounded different, much more confident.

She's lost weight, Heather thought. Or maybe it's because her deportment has improved. Her outfit was astonishing. Gone was the nervous secretary, now a leather-clad figure in a scarlet jump-suit. It accentuated her curves, a single zipper running from the throat, down round the crotch and up between her buttocks to fasten at the nape. The height of her heels made her calves bunch, lengthened her thighs and emphasied her hips. She was lightly swishing a bull-whip, then running the long thongs through her black-gloved fingers.

'Fun and games?' Xanthia enquired, and stalked over to the cubicle, staring down at the naked man tethered by his wrists and ankles.

'Oh, yes. I found out that he was one of those self-centred individuals who thought only of his own pleasure,' Julie answered sternly, bending over and tweaking his nipples. 'He needs a lesson in manners.'

'Dear me, yes,' Xanthia nodded in agreement. 'I hope you're not permitting him to come?'

'Certainly not!' Julie sharply rapped his penis which had started to rise from its bed of hair. 'Down, boy!' she cried.

The man, a good-looking, middle-aged individual who was a tycoon in daily life, gave vent to a strangled whimper. 'You're cruel,' he complained.

'Nonsense!' Julie snapped. 'You've been a very naughty boy – and I think you need punishing. My friends have come along to make sure you get it.'

Xanthia stood where he could not avoid seeing her, legs spread so that the deep pink wings of her labia were visible. Then she inserted a finger, worked it inside her, withdrew it and spread its wetness over her clit.

Her eyes were on Heather all the while, as if to say – now you can orgasm. Heather opened her bodice, cupping and bouncing her breasts, teasing the nipples into points. Then she hoisted

115

one leg on to a high stool near the couch, and kept the other braced on the floor. Her skirt was rolled up to her waist, her bottom bare, her sex open and gleaming with moisture. Her fingertips started playing around her centre, which needed scant encouragement, swelling at once.

'Won't you touch each other, girls? I'd like to watch you do it,' the man panted, writhing on the couch, his penis out of control again, standing up straight as a flag-pole.

'Be quiet!' Julie reprimanded. 'We're doing this for our enjoyment, not yours. You are permitted to watch, but not touch. Maybe later I might relieve you, but then again, I might change my mind.'

His moans were of a man in an extremity of torment. Julie grinned, took the clasp of her zip and slowly allowed it to run down. Her breasts popped out of the opening, her belly was revealed, then the thick fair down covering her pubis. The bound man stared goggle-eyed at the deep, pink groove between the fur.

'D'you want to finger it?' Julie asked, so close to him now.

'Yes – I do. Untie me.' He was sweating, and as she moistened her finger at her juicy fount and rubbed it across his nipples, so his penis convulsed.

'It's impatient, isn't it?' Xanthia commented, in control as her hand continued to stimulate her bud.

The three women looked down at that large, pulsing, red-capped cock, which seemed to be weeping from its one eye. 'Shall we attend to it?' Julie asked them, keeping up the friction on her engorged nub.

'Later, maybe. First I'm going to come,' and Xanthia, caught in the compelling rhythm.

'Wait for me!' Heather cried. 'Can't we all three come together?'

Julie was into this game, handling herself with the expertise which comes through years of masturbation. Timing their strokes, they succeeded in this endeavour, all three climaxing within a hair's breadth of the other.

'I'm there – wonderful!' Xanthia gasped.

'It's coming! Yes! Yes!' exclaimed Heather.

'Here it is! Ah – ah—' Julie yelled.

'My God, do it to me!' the man begged, the sweat trickling down his hairy body, his penis in a monumental state of arousal. 'What is it with you? Are you Lesbians?'

Xanthia was the first to recover herself. 'I can't speak for the others, but I'm bi-sexual. You'd like to watch Lesbians at it? You'd be lucky! They wouldn't have a man within a mile when they're making it together.'

'Really?' He expressed nervous surprise, over-awed by these powerful, self-sufficent woman. 'I thought they'd let me watch them – maybe join in.'

'Two women, one man. That's a common enough fantasy, but an illusion. Most men find it hard enough to service one.' Julie had a ruthless glint in her eyes.

'You'd like to show them what they're missing, d'you mean?' Xanthia leaned over the man, her breasts swinging forward so that his cock was embedded between those solid, golden orbes.

He was pushing up and down with his hips, straining against the bonds, desperately hoping to spend himself against her before she moved away. A vain hope.

She gave his bursting penis a disdainful flick with a bronzed fingernail. 'And what *would* they be missing, eh? This puny object?'

117

Heather began to feel rather sorry for him. He was in an obviously distressed state and Julie had probably been flaunting herself in front of him for ages, protracting his torture. Then she remembered Ragnar, and her own frustration – Charles, too, and her pity disappeared.

'I want to mount him,' she said suddenly, needing to be filled after the hot stream of release that had convulsed her during orgasm.

'Why not?' Xanthia was behind Heather, hands on her protegée's haunches, gently kneading the dimpled flesh, opening her legs, fingers rejoicing in the damp avenue that connected with her mound.

Heather climbed above the man and carefully lowered herself on his quivering prick. She rocked gently, feeling it pulse against her inner walls. Up and down she rose, but, when he began to buck and grunt, Xanthia stopped her.

At this signal, Heather rose off the pulsing member and Xanthia took her place. Her movements were harder, like steel which might close on and snap his shaft. He gasped, pushed into her and she let him believe that he was to be allowed to explode in the sharp release of climax. His eyes were tight shut, mouth gaping, seeking that final push which would tip him into esctasy.

It was then that Julie murmured, 'He's not to have it.'

'You're right.' Xanthia dismounted.

The cool air was on his skin, his penis at a dejected angle, almost beginning to droop. There were tears in his eyes. 'Damn you,' he muttered. 'Come back – one of you. It's not fair to leave me like this.'

'Are you whingeing?' Julie took command. 'How dare you complain? Let me have a go!'

She was on him, her spiky heels scratching his

sides. Down she plunged on to his organ, which had stiffen in response. She rode him hard, which combined with the humiliation they had heaped on him, made it difficult for him to come no matter how much he ached to do so. Staring down at his straining body, his arched throat and agonised face, she looked back over the years, remembering every man who had betrayed her.

Deliberately, she denied him the rhythm he needed to bring him off. Then, in one swift movement, she slid away, leaving him groaning, poised on the edge, unable to achieve fulfilment.

Heather, Xanthia and Julie, arms linked, considered the furious man for a moment. 'If you won't finish it, then at least unbind me,' he demanded angrily.

'You know that you enjoy it really. Isn't this what you're here for – to be denied and abused by women?' Julie unsnapped the handcuffs, side-stepping as he tried to grab her.

He glowered at them, stretching out to untie his ankles. 'Slags!' he snarled.

'Now, now – if you talk so rudely to us, we won't come out to play tomorrow,' Julie reproved.

She leaned forward and kissed him on the cheek. 'Why are you so cruel?' he grumbled.

'I'm not.' She rubbed her breasts against his shoulder, took his tool in her hand, gave the head a quick suck, then withdrew, adding with an impish grin, 'You're free now. Think about us as you jerk off.'

They turned towards the door, three leather-clad goddesses after whom he looked longingly as he held his balls in one hand and started to caress his penis with the other.

Chapter Seven

THE AFTERNOON WAS hot, but not unpleasantly so for those who had nothing to do but idle their time away. Heather, attired in a white lawn Edwardian gown, such as might have been worn by a genteel lady around 1901, had arrived to play croquet on the green velvet sward behind Tostavyn Grange.

It's like a scene from a Merchant Ivory movie, she thought, aware that her long skirts made a seductive frou-frou as she walked. I wouldn't be surprised of one of our Oscar-winning English actors suddenly appeared, playing the butler.

The area was shaded by Spanish oaks and cedars, the sky was cloudless and somewhere, high up, larks soared and dipped, so far away that their song could hardly be heard. A hammock was slung from the branches of a monkey-puzzle tree, and a young man in white flannels and striped blazer reclined there, panama hat resting nonchalantly on his chest.

Close by sat a colonel – an uncle or somesuch. He occupied a canvas-seated campaign chair, a stout, rubicund man with a grey waxed moustache twirled into fierce military points either side of his upper lip. His neatly barbered hair was winged with grey at the temples.

Though supposedly keeping an eye on the youngsters and acting as a chaperon, his eyes lingered on the girls lasciviously. When Heather passed him, he reached out a hand and patted the small of her back, then pushed into the crease between her buttocks, saying, 'Afternoon, m'dear. Your mama has detailed me to look after you. You may be betrothed to Cedric,' and he had indicated the hammock-user, 'but that don't give him leave to make free with you.'

Nor you either, you dirty-minded old goat! Heather thought, stepping aside as she smiled sweetly at him and replied, 'I don't know what you mean, Uncle.'

'Of course you don't, my innocent little pet,' he leered, smoothing his moustache with one hand while the other slipped beneath the newspaper spread over his lap. Heather stalked away.

A maid-servant, decorously clad in black with a frilled white apron and a cap with streamers floating at the back, served tea from a silver Queen Anne pot. This, along with delicate china cups and a plate of iced fancy-cakes, was placed on a pristine lace-edged cloth. As she bent over the cane table, the Colonel touched her up. Heather heard her gasp and murmur, 'Oh, sir, d'you think you should do that? Not now, sir – but I can meet you in the shrubbery later.'

So much for Edwardian double-standards, Heather thought as she strolled across the lawn. How can I pretend to be innocent after the feverish experience of the past days. I've been taught to masturbate, had a doctor put his cock in me, have discovered that I like watching women frigging, then André has penetrated me, that trusted, family friend – though he didn't come, it's true. There was the West Indian guy, the

Viking, and I helped Julie with her SM games. Now Xanthia is demanding that I put this from my mind and concentrate on maidenly thoughts, prurient though they may be.

Two other elegant young men and a pretty girl, as beautifully attired as Heather, were her opponents. Tock went her mallet against the wooden ball. There were approving cried of, 'Roquet! Well done, Lady Heather!'

It seemed she was doing rather well, in this, her first ever attempt. She wondered about the other people there. Were they simply Xanthia's actors? Or were they guests? That wily woman wasn't in evidence to question. She had not appeared that day. A message had been delivered with Heather's early morning tea, along with the outfit she was now wearing.

It had read: 'Variety being the spice of life, you're off on another adventure. I'm sending a maid to help you dress. Stays are a devil to lace on one's own. She'll take you to your destination. I know from your impressive acting ability that you'll slip neatly into the role of a modest Edwardian miss who is, in reality, burning up inside with curiosity about that forbidden subject – sex. Follow my instructions to the letter, and I promise you another mind-blowing escapade. I've enclosed a rough scenario. Oh, one last thing – keep your finger off you-know-where. I want you to be in a state of galloping frustration, ready, hot and jumping with eagerness.'

Clothes – so many of them. How on earth did the women survive? Heather wondered. High summer, and she was shrouded in a chemise, corsets that pinched her waist, drawers that came to her knees, even though they were slit at the crotch and had a buttoned flap at the back, two lacy petticoats, black woollen stockings and tight patent shoes with Louis heels. On top of this was the dress, full-skirted, with a fearsomely restrictive bodice and leg-o'-mutton sleeves. And there were the obligatory white kid gloves.

Was it possible to indulge in sexual activities dressed like that? Were the open gussetted knickers the answer?

Even as the thought crossed her mind, she was aware of that naked area between her legs. Bending from the waist to take aim with her mallet, she could feel her damp, secret lips, and when she remembered Xanthia's written words forbidding her to touch herself, so her bud commenced to throb.

Cedric, rising gracefully from his resting-place, idled over to stand beside her. He lifted the monocle that he wore on a black satin ribbon round his neck and regarded her through it.

'You're a natural croquet player, little thing,' he remarked in a languid, patronising voice.

He was handsome in a refined, effete manner, his hair parted in the middle and slicked back with macassar oil, and gleaming like a satin cap. The blazer, his straw hat, those narrow white trousers, a shirt with a starched collar, the silver watch-chain spanning his waistcoat all indicated a person of conservative views. Did Cedric do rude things to the housemaids, as Uncle obviously did? Heather mused.

Glancing sideways at his crotch, she saw the plump outline of his penis to the left of the fly buttons. Small, as yet. Would it get bigger if he kissed her?

Get him to do it, the script had said.

Heather threw down her mallet. 'I'm tired of this stupid game!' she said pettishly. 'It's too hot! Can't we go for a walk, Cedric? It will be cool among the trees.'

'If that's what you want, my dear.' He crooked his elbow and she slipped a gloved hand through it.

She nodded coolly to the others, murmuring her excuses. 'We'll continue play another time. Thank you for showing me how.'

A tree-shaded avenue, the sunlight dappling through the leaves. Within seconds, the couple were hidden from view. Cedric, panama tilted at a jaunty angle, a walking-cane in his hand, took Heather along a path that led between lush rhododendron bushes where the heavy pinkish flowers drooped in the embrace of shiny green foliage. There was a gamey smell in the air – thyme and camomile, damp earth, rotting undergrowth – vaguely reminiscent of the sweet aroma of sex.

They followed a stream that bubbled over flat, dark pebbles to where it cascaded, a natural waterfall, into a pool. Here they stopped in a hidden den, obscurred from view. Now, Heather decided and, taking a deep breath so that her breasts lifted provocatively, she turned to him.

'Would you like to kiss me, Cedric?' she asked, her face raised to his, eyes enquiring under her long lashes, subjecting him to the most bewitching look she could muster.

He paused, stumbled over the words. 'Of course I would. I suppose it's quite the proper thing to do. After all, you are my fiancé.'

He took off his hat and removed his monocle, while she waited, eyes closed, lips puckered. She felt him close in, but instead of his mouth fastening on hers, he merely brushed her cheek.

Heather's lids flew open. She glared at him, remembering her lines. 'That's not a real kiss!'

It wasn't hard to pretend. The secluded spot, the gurgling sound of water, the pungent odours

124

of wet vegetation were rousing her. She could feel her nipples burning against her chemise, those linen drawers rubbing against her cleft as she moved. Here she was, alone with a man, and he was behaving like a prig!

Quarrel with him. Those were her instructions.

'But, darling girl,' Cedric spluttered. 'We mustn't! We're not married!'

'Damn marriage, and damn you!' she shouted. 'If *you* don't want to kiss me on the lips, then I'll find someone who does!'

Holding her skirts up in one hand, she flounced off, taking the path that led to the stables, aware of Cedric calling after her, though he didn't follow. He, too, has his orders, she thought. Xanthia has given them and he daren't disobey.

The stable-yard was cobbled, an ancient place of stone-walled outbuildings. A couple of tabby cats were stretched sensually on the edge of a grey slate roof, yellow eyes half closed as they watched the doves preening on the cote while, with feline cunning, they pretended to be snoozing. A fulsome odour rose from the straw and the manure heaped in corners, and a groom led a horse from one of the stalls as Heather stormed across.

'You want to ride, your ladyship?' he asked in a country accent, a tow-headed lad who smiled at her cheekily, while the animal fidgeted slightly, hooves sounding hollow on the cobbles.

'I do!' she snapped, eyeing the boy up and down.

He wasn't quite her style – too gangling by far – though the chest glimpsed through the gap in his open-necked shirt was tanned, and there was a promising fullness between the thighs of his corduroy breeches. The soles of his hob-nailed boots were covered in muck.

'If I may make so bold, milady, you ain't dressed for it,' he remarked, and there was a certain rustic charm about him, an innocent sensuality, a cockiness that hinted at inexperience coupled with a ragingly salacious interest in the opposite sex.

Was he a virgin? Had he ever come, apart from wanking? The idea of surprising him in the stable loft, breeches gaping open as he lay in the hay, hands busy stimulating his strong young cock, stirred something within Heather. It would be fun to teach him. Her love-bud awakened, secret lips starting to engorge, the glans just inside the opening of her vulva giving forth a clear, slippery secretion.

'Keep your opinions to yourself, Thomas!' she said coldly. 'Help me up.'

He bent, cupped his hands, and Heather placed a foot in them, rising effortlessly and settling into the demure side-saddle position. Even so, she was aware of her labia grazing her petticoats, which formed a tiresome barrier between her genitals and the warm hardness of leather.

She was accustomed to riding astride, an experienced horsewoman who had been worried, till now, at the uncomfortable ache that had pervaded her loins when her tight jodpurs rubbed against her, the bumping motion jarring her clitoris. Now that she knew the cause of this discomfort and its remedy, she smiled as she wondered if this was the reason why horse-riding became an obsession with young girls, and indeed with older women, too.

Did this account for the rosy cheeks and bright eyes of her friends when they returned from a hard gallop? Had they been giving themselves orgasms on the way? It was an intriguing speculation and Heather couldn't wait to see if such a thing was possible.

The groom stepped back, smiling. 'Have a good ride, milady.'

'I will, Thomas.' My God, how cool and dignified, when in reality her nub was begging for relief.

Heather unpinned her wide-brimmed hat and threw it to him, then rode out of the yard and across the drive. It was a glorious afternoon, a few fluffy clouds dotting the azure sky, the flowerbeds a dazzle of colour. When she reached a white-painted fence, she saw that the gate was already open. She rode through the parklands and out across the estate, giving her mount his head, her hair tumbling about her shoulders in wanton profusion.

Ahead she could see a copse, with a golden meadow beyond. This was the chosen venue for the next phase of the game. They circled the tuft of trees. Heather crouched low against the flying mane, the wind plastering strands of her hair across her mouth, the speed of their flight exaggerating the excitement of those powerful flanks rising and falling beneath her. She relished the maleness of the animal, the reek of leather and the stench of his foam-flecked haunches a potent adjunct to the tumultuous lust that was making her sex ripe and juicy.

They cleared the woods and the horse cantered into the meadows. There Heather tugged on the reins, telling him to halt. Perfect! What a glorious, secret spot. The sun was hot on her neck as she dismounted, after glancing around to make certain that she was unobserved, though she was not too worried. There was an added thrill in suspecting that unseen eyes might be watching her. André perhaps? Or Xanthia? Maybe stimulating each other to full climax.

Heather no longer needed the script to tell her

what to do. She squirmed round and unbuttoned her dress, not an easy task and one which made her sweat. It crumpled in a heap on the buttercup- and clover-starred grass. Next she untied her petticoats and let them drop to join the dress. Those bloody stays! Fingers fumbling with eagerness, breasts longing to be free, she fought with the laces, at last succeeding in undoing them. The constricting garment was flung aside and Heather massaged her freed ribs and lifted her breasts in both hands, paying special attention to the nipples, which immediately formed into tight cones.

Off came the chemise, and she was naked to the waist, stretching and rejoicing in the sunshine. How gloriously untrammelled she felt – and at once the cotton drawers were about her ankles and she stepped out of them. Only the stockings remained, wrinkling down her legs. They, too, were ripped off, and she was completely naked.

'Your turn, old lad,' she said to the horse, and removed the bit from his mouth, then loosened the girth so that the saddle could be lifted away.

He tossed his great head and whinnied.

Heather seized a handful of mane and leapt on to his back, legs spread, straddling his wide sides. At once, fire stabbed up to her nipples at the savage contact between her bare thighs and pussy and his knobbly spine. It pressed into her clit, which almost exploded at the sudden uprush of pleasure.

Heather gave a cry, dug her knees against the beast's sides and urged him into a gallop, giving herself over to the sensations pouring through her loins, belly and breasts. Each stride shifted her backwards and forwards over his rough hide, the friction causing mayhem with her hardened bud. Sometimes squashed, sometimes free from pressure, it quivered and throbbed, the sensation rising sharply as they circled the meadow not once but several times.

Heather clamped her thighs over that broad back, ground herself down so as not to lose that precious chafing on her clit.

'Now!' she cried aloud. 'Now – now! It's coming! Yes – yes! Oh, my God! Let it come. I must have it – I *must!*'

She was rising on a wave of sweet, suffocating anguish – beyond awareness – blind and deaf to everything except that compulsion for orgasm. The horse's coat was slippery with sweat, and this was joined along his backbone by the moisture which spread from her vulva, along that engorged avenue, lubricating her swollen, ultra-sensitive kernel.

She climaxed in a sudden explosion of light and heat, slumping over her mount's withers as he slowed to a walk. The motion maintained a gentle rubbing of that most wonderful of parts, her clitoris, which, still thrumming, started to revive, flooding her nerves with urgent messages.

We'll come again soon, she promised it. We can do it as many times as we want. How many is it possible to achieve, one after the other? Will it say in the *Guinness Book of Records?*

Heather's fingers came down to touch her sacred centre, and the horse, head lowered, started to crop the luscious turf. She slid from his back and, gasping, flung herself down in the long grass, lying absolutely still, apart from one hand fondling her nipples and the other her cleft, eager to work herself up to a climax again.

A figure stepped between her and the sun. She opened her eyes. Someone tall and immensely dark threw his shadow across her. Annoyed at being interrupted, she sat up, hand remaining between her legs. I've become utterly shameless, she thought.

'You've been spying on me!' she cried indignantly, while that melting, liquid feeling pervaded her, her middle finger pressed to her bud.

He smiled, and dropped on his hunkers beside her. 'That's a fine animal you've got there, miss,' he remarked conversationally. 'Damn me if I've seen a finer, if you'll pardon my language. I know a thing or two about horse-flesh.'

'You're a gypsy!' This much was obvious. His swashbuckling good looks stunned her eye and made her womb contract.

'Aye, that's right, miss. I'm a Romany. My name's Jake.'

His hair was black. It twisted into ringlets about an arrogant, swarthy face complete with stubble. Gold hoops glinted in his ears. Peat-brown eyes, strongly marked brows, thick lashes, a firm nose, and the most incredibly sensual red lips. Heather wanted to feel them on her clitoris, wanted him to suck in between his straight white teeth, wanted those lean, tanned hands to lift and hold her breasts.

'Well, Jake – I could ask you what you're doing on my father's land. Has he given permission?' She adopted the high-flown tone of the lady of the manor, difficult though it was with the heat of lust consuming her.

'The Squire? Oh, aye, he never denies us the right to pitch camp in the Top Spinney. We've been doing it for years.' He grinned at her impudently as if reading her thoughts, then pulled up a blade of grass and wedged it between his lips. 'You the Squire's daughter?'

'Yes, I'm Lady Heather.' She was staring,

mesmerised, at his wide shoulders straining against the white, collarless shrit. It was open to the waist and, seeing the dark curling mat of hair on his chest, she wanted to plunge her fingers into it, locate his nipples and tweak them.

'And what're you doing out here without your clothes on, milady?' he asked, eyed devouring her breasts, her belly, the damp fluffy wedge of her pubis. 'Seemed like you was bringing yourself off against that nag's back. I can do better than that for you. I'd love to stroke and kiss you, lick your juices, rub your pussy-lips with my cock-head.'

'I was simply riding,' she answered lamely, recalling the intense spasm of pleasure that had thundered through her, and which were starting to rise again at his crude and inflammatory words.

'I wish you'd ride me like that,' he said in a dusky undertone that stippled her skin with goose-bumps. 'I'd get ramrod hard if I felt your gorgeous tits bumping my spine, and your randy quim grinding against my arse.'

Heather could not prevent herself from glancing down to where he lay on the grass beside her. His long legs were apart, one knee raised, the other outstretched. He wore dark grey moleskin trousers, but even these could not hide the promising bulge that betrayed the presence of a hardening phallus.

Reaching over, she unbuttoned him. He made no attempt to stop her. His large, eager tool rose through the gap, brushing against her fingers as it emerged from its prison.

She grasped it, working the foreskin up and down over the swollen knob that shone like polished glass, till she was rewarded with the sticky feel of lubrication.

'Not too much, milady,' he warned, groaning

even as he started to buck. 'Or it'll be over before we've started.'

He gripped her by the back of the neck and pulled her lips down to his. His tongue thrust between her teeth, thick, wet and smooth, caressing the inside of her mouth, while his free hand toyed with each up-thrusting breast in turn. She was ready, wanting him then and there, but he paused, smiled into her passion-drugged eyes and said, 'I know a place, milady. Come with me.'

'Is it in the open?' She wanted to be fucked out there under the blue sky – as free as air – as free as a vagabond like Jake.

'Yes.' He leapt to his feet, hauled her up against him. 'I could take you to my *vardo*, but it's too near the camp. The tribe would object to you, but I've always wanted to fuck a *gorgio* girl.'

'They'd object – to *me*?' Heather was surprised, though it was hard to concentrate on anything with his arm around her, a hand supporting one breast.

He gave a deep, throaty chuckle. 'Don't give yourself airs, Lady Heather. My father's a Duke of Little Egypt and I'm a prince. Oh, no – Roms shouldn't mate with *gorgios*. It's not good for the blood-line. They've already fixed me up with a pure gypsy girl. She wants to be my *monisha*, and give me many strong, healthy sons and daughters.'

I don't like this bit of the movie, Heather thought, even as she wound her arms round his neck and burrowed her fingers in his long curls. I want it to be real. That's the trouble. I want to have him take me away in his wagon, forget his tribe and that girl they've chosen. My emotions are getting involved with this one, my heart as well as my loins. I didn't realise till now how much I wanted an adventurer or just what kind of

132

a rebel I am myself.

Getting a grip, she forced herself to remember that this was only an illusion – an afternoon's entertainment. Jake wasn't really a gypsy. He was probably an actor, hired by Xanthia, who'd be back in his flat in London in less than a week, waiting for his agent to phone with the offer of further work. Next time I see him, he'll be advertising aftershave or 501s or high performance cars on TV, she thought, but the dream had hold of her and she wanted to exist in it, if only for a little while.

She gathered up her clothes and, his arm circling her waist, the horse's rein held in his other fist, they left the meadow, the patient beast plodding behind them.

'It's not far,' he murmured in her ear, the tickle of his warm breath playing merry hell with her juices and causing them to dribble down her inside thighs.

He guided her along a path that wound between overhanging branches, culminating in a hidden glade. Small, intimate, it was gloomy but shot across with sudden shafts of golden sunlight. It formed a natural chamber, hedged in on either side by tangled willow, brambles and wild dog-roses.

'You've brought women here before?' she questioned on a burst of jealously that added to her excitement.

He didn't answer for a moment, motioning her down on the mossy green carpet, the remembrance of his cock increasing the deep-seated ache of longing that centred on her clitoris, then spread out in waves over her entire body.

'Not a *gorgio*,' he said at last, dark eyes focusing on her nakedness. 'I told you. You're my first. I've had my *kari* inside the wife of another Rom. He treats her bad, beats her when he's drunk. We had to be careful or I'd have had his knife in my ribs and her face would've been slashed.'

'I thought gypsies were free people,' Heather said, rejoicing in his good looks as he settled beside her. She found it hard to resist the temptation to release his penis, which was once again imprisoned in his trousers.

He laughed. 'Oh, no, milady – no more free than you and yours. We've our taboos and traditions, too.'

Heather wriggled against him; she wanted action, not talk. She was nude, he wasn't – and she wanted to see his body, his phallus, was burning to study it again, to compare its size and length with the others she'd known recently.

'I'd like you to take off your clothes,' she purred, in her most seductive voice.

He grinned, stood up. 'My shirt can go, but not my trousers. You'll never get a gypsy to do that. Not you, though, you're not ashamed to let me look at your *minge*.'

'You use such fancy words,' she laughed, one hand at the back of her head, sweeping up and supporting her long, thick hair. '*Kari, minge*—'

'They're Romany, but they mean the same thing – cock, cunt—'

He looked at her, saw the drooping red lips, the hooded eyelids that made it seem she was in a dream. His fingers worked on the buttons of his shirt, and then she rose to finish the job, sliding it from his wide, muscular shoulders. He shuddered as they curled in the thick mat of hair that covered his chest, circled the pectorals, moved closer to the small brown nipples, then pinched them gently.

Heather, her body pressed close, following the lines of his, could feel the hardness and heat of his arousal through his trousers. She bent in one lithe movement, and her lips closed on his right nipple, sucking it strongly.

He started, a drawn-out moan escaping from his throat, the expression of an intense need that demanded satisfaction. Then Heather knew that this was going to be a straight forward fuck with an unsophisticated man. She must not expect slow, lingering delight. She wondered if he would be rough, looked at his hands, which were hard, tanned and dirty. Would they hurt her? Or would they prove to have natural sensitivity?

Her breathing was ragged as he raised her, and his kiss was at first as light as spring rain, before he became more demanding. He leaned his back against the bole of a tree, and pulled her against him. His tongue darted in and out of her mouth, those large hands cupping the fleshy spheres of her breasts as she arched her spine and lifted them high, nipples begging for the touch of his thumbs.

Surreptitiously, she edged her legs a little further apart, feeling the stab of pine needles on the soles of her bare feet, the prickling sensation sending shocks of pain and pleasure up into her thighs and stiff clit. She sighed and sighed into his mouth, her own tongue answering his with burning jabs of its own.

Removing his lips from hers, he lowered his curly head and grasped one nipple, sucking and biting it, winding his tongue round the pebble-hard teat with an urgency that numbed her mind. He found her mouth again and slowly, still holding her, slid down the scabrous trunk that was covered in patches of yellow-grey lichen. Heather gave herself over to him, this great dark man, this wild creature from the woods, who could do with her as he willed. She coiled against him, eager as a virgin bride.

The dell was hot with the sun held between the high trees like a bowl of liquid gold. In its glow, in the pervading mystic green, Heather's senses swam. Jake, so handsome, so primitive in his needs, was a man seeking a mate – driven to fill her with his spunk, to pump it into her womb to ensure the survival of his tribe.

And she wanted that – oh, so much! To throw away ambition, to forget civilisation and all its empty vanities – cast it all aside and become a nomad. Jake and her, god and goddess of the woodlands, coupling on the soil to produce chubby, olive-skinned babies.

She fell with him to the ground, intoxicated by the perfume of crushed grass and wild flowers, her pelvis thrust towards him as he sought her epicentre. His finger plunged into her vagina, while his lips were at her breast again, sucking with the avidity of a hungry infant starved for too long of its mother's milk.

She wriggled, trying to position her hips so that his finger would leave her vulva and slide up to where she ached for its touch – on her clitoris, now pulsating with unsatisfied need.

'You want your love-bud stroked? Is that it, milady?' he murmured on a hoarse, thickened tone. 'Then you shall have it, my darling.'

Just for a moment, he stared, entranced, at the smooth, clean lines of her flat belly, the hip bone making peaks on either side. His concentrated gaze on the visual reaches of her sex exacerbated the lust pounding through her. How wonderful it was to have him examine the glossy darkness of her triangle, a thick puff of fur, and that plump hillock which rose so high and fell away so steeply to the mystery concealed below.

She bent her knees, letting her thighs drift open, revealing the petals of her pink, honey-steeped labia, pressing the lips apart with one hand, so that her clitoris, solid as a pea, rose out of its hood.

Jake gasped, then bent. He pushed his tongue into her navel, moving it round and round till Heather voiced her pleasure in a series of little cries and whimpers. Next her pressed his mouth to the dark hair of her mound while he passed his hands over the insides of her thighs, caressing them, moving closer to her hottest spot.

Heather was becoming desperate. 'Touch me there.' She took hold of his hand and pushed it to the pleasure point between her plump love-lips.

The shock of the contact between her sensitive bud and his harsh, dry finger was almost too much, taking the edge off ecstasy. It was too hard, too intense. Even though she was poised agonisingly on the brink, she knew she'd never topple over like that. Quivering and vulnerable without its furled cowl, her clit required the most delicate treatment. Would a gypsy like him know how to give it, massaging with butterfly-light touch, taking her to the highest peak of exquisite sensation that would force her to fly from the precipice?

He grunted, kissed her lips, then slid down till he lay between her thighs, taking his mouth to her vagina. He turned his head till his lips were alongside her secret ones. So much fluid now, almost too much – his saliva, her flooding juices. Along her cleft he went with that clever, miraculous tongue – finding the tiny bud, tasting it, teasing it, then settling down to a soft, sucking motion.

Such unselfishness astonished Heather. In the midst of her extremity, she dug her fingers into his crisp, raven curls, then kneaded his wide, tanned, naked shoudlers with her fists. He groaned as he tormented her clit, then stopped the rhythm, drawing his tongue back into his mouth so that the chill air played over that tortured bud.

'I want to make it last for you,' he whispered.

'Don't stop!' she yelled, her hands harsh on his scalp, nails digging in, hating herself for begging, but forced to. 'Lick me – you must lick me!'

He laughed and obeyed, lapping the hot fluid that flowed from her, lapping at her straining bud that jumped at the joy of his returning tongue. Her eyelids fluttered shut. Her lips were open wide, red and lustrous. The waves were crashing over her now, each one lifting her towards that treasured peak. She was up – up – peaking, reaching it. The tingle started in the tips of her toes, rolling in waves up her legs, into her spine, through her breasts, loins, the core of her very being, growing into an orgasm so powerful that she felt as if her body was disintegrating into fragments to be scattered among the stars.

While the convulsions were still undulating through her, Jake rose to his knees, positioned himself between her thighs and thrust his enormous shaft into her vagina. She cried aloud as her inner walls closed over the long, thick trunk of it, feeling the head pressing against her cervix, almost hurting her with its size. He was way beyond thought now, braced on his arms, head up, his expression that of a saint undergoing martyrdom.

He drove his cock into her again and again, until she felt that final jerk that heralded the stream of warm semen that burst from him, bedewing her inner core. The neck of her womb contracted, dipping down to skim that milky pool, sucking it back into itself.

He held her tight, trying to prolong the ecstasy

and, when the wildness had faded from his eyes, he sank his head against his breasts, his breathing quieting. Bruised flowers, mangled grass, her own sweat and his, the powerful, sexy smell of their mingled body fluids – Heather wished she could bottle it up and keep it for times when she was alone and no man lay in her arms.

Chapter Eight

THEY WALKED BACK through the woods in the hush of early evening. Heather had dressed again, with Jake's help, though this had led inevitably to further copulation, his prick stiffening again at the sight of her in stays.

Heather shivered as she relived every passion-packed moment. How could she forget with their mingled juices seeping from her vagina with every step she took? The shadows were lengthening, a bluish haze spreading through the trees, the silence broken only by the cries of circling rooks seeking night-time roosts.

When they arrived at the gate leading into the grounds, Jake handed over the reins, his fingers lingering on hers. They stood silently, the magnetic force of their desire making them lean into one another, then she said, 'I don't suppose we'll meet again.'

She wanted to touch his cheek, to feel the stubble prickling her fingers, to melt into his arms and have his hard cock nudging her belly. Only a massive effort at self-control prevented her from lifting her skirts and clamping her legs round his thigh, brazen clitoris begging for more delicious friction.

Dear me, you've embraced this role with a vengeance! she lectured herself. You're not Lady Chatterley and he isn't her lover, that bloody game-keeper, Mellors. Pull yourself together, girl!

'Good night, Jake,' she said, turning away reluctantly, every nerve taut.

'Good night, milady,' he answered, with a touch of irony.

Tears misted her sight as she walked on resolutely, half expecting to feel him behind her, slipping his hands around under her armpits to cup her breasts, lifting them in a lingering, loving way. Nothing happened.

She felt a sharp pang of loss. As she walked, she tried to get her jumbled emotions together, making an inventory of what had taken place so far.

OK, so André and Xanthia had awakened her sensuality. She now knew how to please men and, more important, how to please herself. But was this all there was to it? Must she share their cynical view that one penis was as good as another? Was it really necessary to close her heart to love? There was no doubt that her romantic illusions had taken a nose-dive.

She heaved a sigh, bidding her dreams goodbye, and it was difficult to let them go amidst such an enchanting setting. The sky was a limpid turquoise, washed with violet, indigo clouds banking to sweep their dark wings over everything once the sun had vanished beyond the horizon. The pale half moon that had hung, ghostlike, in the heavens all day was gathering luminosity, attended by a retinue of stars.

It was an evening calculated to encourage dreams and, as Heather reached the terrace she met Julie, who was also idling along staring at the view. The rapt expression on her face contrasted incongruously with her warlike apparel. She was wearing a short white kilt, an engraved metal breastplate complete with moulded boobs, greaves strapped to her legs over thonged sandals, and a huge, crested helmet. She carried a short sword and round shield.

'Hi there, and what are you supposed to be?' Heather asked with a smile as they stopped in front of each other.

'I'm an Amazon warrior,' Julie answered, lifting the helmet from her blonde hair, sweaty tendrils sticking to her dirt-streaked temples. 'I led my women against enemy men this afternoon. We won, of course, and have been screwing our prisoners – just like the Amazons did when they wanted to get pregnant. They kept the girl babies, and sent the boys back to their fathers. They didn't need men, you see – only for procreation. They governed their territory, fought off intruders, had sex with each other and managed beautifully, or so the legend goes.'

'How very civilised,' Heather replied, though she sighed again as she seated herself on the edge of a stone balustrade, the coldness chilling her backside. 'Did you enjoy it?'

'I loved the battle, and being able to take my pick of the cocks on offer,' Julie enthused. 'But it was damned hot!'

She unbuckled her steel corselet and massaged her emerging breasts, those fine, upstanding spheres which always gave her a somewhat top-heavy appearance. Beneath she wore a plain white tunic that clung to every tempting curve of her generous body, outlining the hard brown nipples pressed against the sweat-soaked linen.

'Did you rape your prisoners?' Heather watched Julie in fascination, yielding to the hot desire roused by the notion of touching those puckered teats.

'We did. It *is* possible to rape men, you know, though I can't say these put up much resistance.' Julie sat down opposite Heather, absent-mindedly caressing her pussy as she gloated over the snapshots in her mind. 'We dragged them back in chains to our camp. When we saw any we fancied, some of the girls held them down, threatening to cut off their nuts if they didn't lie quiet, while the rest of us gave them a thorough seeing-to.'

'Did it work?' From where Heather sat, she could look up Julie's pleated kilt, see her rounded knees and plump inner thighs, and the fuzzy linten hair that covered the juicy crevice beneath.

She wanted to touch it, her own nectar seeping out, mind overflowing with images of those preoccupied brothel-girls working themselves to orgasm on the night of her initiation. She'd never yet masturbated a woman, and her tongue and hands itched to try it.

'Sure thing.' Julie's finger was pressing her clitoris in thoughtful fashion. 'In no time at all they were horny as hell, pricks to attention. I can still taste their cock-juice. Makes me feel randy again.'

Heather swallowed. 'And this is how the Amazons kept the tribe going. I hope it doesn't work for you, Julie, and you find yourself in the pudding club.'

Julie laughed, eyes slightly off-focus as she gloated over the afternoon's delights, secret place so wet and steamy that Heather could smell it. 'No chance of that, thanks to modern technology.' Then she stopped fingering herself, a serious droop to her cushiony Cupid's bow lips. 'I'd like kiddies one day, though.'

'When the illusive Prince Charming comes

along to sweep you up on his big white horse?' Heather asked wistfully, her body demanding that she return to Jake's arms. She ached to feel his shaft driving into her, expanding her vagina to the limit.

Julie's blue eyes were misted over. 'You understand, don't you? You're not a heartless cow, like Xanthia. I'm tired of whipping blokes. I enjoyed it at first, but now it's a bit of a drag.'

'Like me, you want to fall in love,' Heather whispered, and she shivered as a breeze rushed over the terrace. How good it would be to have Jake warming her. 'I met a gypsy in the woods today, and he was wonderful. He had a body to die for.'

'Girls! Girls! What's all this silly talk?' Xanthia burst in on them, as tall and imperious as if she were an Amazon queen herself, even though she wore a clinging poppy-red velvet gown of French cut and sophistication. 'Haven't you yet learned that if you get hung up on men they treat you like shit?'

'Surely there must be some nice ones somewhere?' Heather protested, rather ashamed of betraying her feelings.

'Perhaps.' Xanthia sounded unconvinced, moving across the herring-bone patterned tiles. Her gorgeous bare legs and tanned mound were revealed momentarily as her skirt, split to the thigh on each side, fell apart with the length of her stride.

She was intimidatingly confident, placing an arm round the shoulders of her novices and hugging them. 'I can see that I've left you to your own devices too long,' she continued. 'We'll have to do something about that, won't we? Can't have you drifting into old habits of thinking. You fancy being a man's slave? Well, my dears, let's see how you enjoy the reality.'

They dined in her suite. She told them not to bother to change their clothes as this would be done later. The richly sombre apartment was candle-lit, orange points stabbing the darkness from floor-standing girandoles. The sumptuous heliotrope drapes shut out the night. An overpowering smell of insense wafted from chafing dishes around whose antique bases bronze serpents coiled. There was another odour, too – strong and heady – breathed out from the trumpet-like blossoms of huge white flowers with thick, fleshy leaves and flamboyant coppery stamens.

Samir waited at table, the food arriving by lift and wheeled in on heated trolleys. He still wore black, as dignified as a Persian vizier, though his mistress treated him as if he were a household pet, running an intimate finger down the baton of his manhood clearly defined by the thin cotton of his tight trousers as he leaned over to serve her.

'Samir, you'll prepare the Turkish rooms,' she announced from her place at the head of the table, where she was seated in a thronelike chair of great age and value.

'Your wish is my command, *sitt*,' he replied, hands to his head and heart.

Music rippled through the air, adding to the *Arabian Night's* ambience. Flutes trilled, drums beat – a voice wailed, slightly discordant – creating a dreamy atmosphere. These harmonies conjured up tantalising visions of semi-nude belly dancers, bejewelled *houris* with supple waists and jiggling breasts, their movements blatantly suggestive as they gyrated their hips.

The meal, served on gilt-rimmed, exotically decorated Spode ware, was superb. Little parcels of cooked vines leaves containing delectably spiced chicken and rice sent out wisps of fragrant steam, and there was an amazing amount of small bowls into which the diner could dip as fancy dictated. Ornate carafes of wine stood between the seven-branched candelabra that ranged the length of the table.

'Drink, Heather,' Xanthia said, in her fruity contralto voice. 'Drink and forget every preconceived idea you ever had.'

Samir filled a shining goblet with ritualistic solemnity, handing it to Heather. The liquid tasted sweet as honey, yet had a slightly bitter undertone. She could hear Julie giggling as she described in graphic detail her sport with one of her prisoners—

'You should've seen the size of his dong! I've never come across anything like it. It must've been all of twelve inches long. As for his balls—'

Then Xanthia's reply, threaded with lazy amusement. 'Really? Maybe I'll have them all stripped and find out who it was. I could do with a big one like that at this very moment.'

There was something the matter with Heather's eyes. Xanthia and Julie seemed suspended in space, pale faces floating against the darkness. The room throbbed, or maybe it was just her loins. The lust that possessed her was overwhelming. How much longer must she wait? And for whom? Already she was finding it hard to remember Jake's face, if not his penis.

She wriggled restlessly in her chair, feeling the ridge in the centre of the seat digging into her cleft. Her juices oozed and dampness soaked the open edges of her Edwardian drawers. She tried to angle her hips to get that much needed pressure on her swelling bud. Everything swam, changing size, shrinking, enlarging – and Samir was watching her with dark, glittering eyes. She saw his smiling lips, the teeth long and white.

Suddenly Xanthia's voice bounced off the vaulted ceiling, loud and clearly enunciated. 'Come with me, Heather. Julie, go with Samir.'

The dizzying sensation made Heather sway as she stood up, but it didn't matter. Xanthia understood and would satisfy her cravings. All she had to do was follow where she led.

Night closed in, wrapping the house in mystery. Silence seemed to drift on the perfume of flowers from the garden beyond the windows as Heather passed into a chamber through a pair of cedarwood doors that were beautifully inlaid with semi-precious stones. She was disoriented, and could not remember how she came to be there. Only one thing stood out diamond-bright – Xanthia had promised her unbridled pleasure, and Heather was keen to embrace it.

Xanthia had gone, but Heather wasn't alone. On either side of the door stood shaven-headed Nubian guards, bare chested, clad in red breeches with huge scimitars in their hands. And right beside her was a most strange figure, straight out of *Aladdin*.

He fixed her with heavy-lidded eyes, the whites glinting like silver in the subdued light, contrasting vividly with his ebony face. He was short and fat, clad in a flowered silk tunic with a broad striped sash girding his paunch. Beneath this she could see the outline of a large appendage that swung beneath his silk pantaloons every time he moved. On his head, he wore a high white hat, and his face was heavily-jowled and brooding, the thick lips petulant, the nose broad and flat.

He carried a whip and, as he looked at Heather, he drew the thong through his fingers thoughtfully, wearing a diabiolical expression of lust and cruelty.

Was he a eunuch? she wondered, trying to see. She had read somewhere that though castrated some of them could still enjoy a modicum of pleasure, usually of the most debased kind. It would be unlikely that he would be permitted anywhere near a harem (and she had guessed by now that this was her location) unless he had been gelded.

'Don't just stand there, you Misbegotten Son of a Camel! Bring the captive forward that I may see her,' came a crisp command, delivered in an authoritative voice with an intriguing foreign accent.

Before Heather realised what was happening she was abruptly hurled to the floor, with the black man hissing in her ear, 'Kneel, woman! Make your obeisance to the Pasha.'

Outraged, stunned and shocked, Heather struggled beneath the pressure of his huge, spatulate hand, muttering, 'I kneel to no one!'

A throaty laugh reached her ears and, dumbfounded, she looked up defiantly, spitting fury. Then every emotion died, to be replaced by a feeling akin to awe.

Immediately before her was a wide bay window. A divan stood beneath the open casements whose gauze curtains stirred gently in the breeze. A man was seated in a nest of brilliantly coloured tapestry cushions, the mouth-piece of a hookah held between his lips. Its base was of silver, rosewater bubbling in a bowl of finest glass, its burner rising like a minaret. Heather breathed deeply of the narcotic smoke, fear over-ridden by the heat that pervaded her secret parts as she found herself being scrutinised by a pair of keen brown eyes.

He was a large man, not tall, but heavily built. His lips curled in a faintly mocking smile. His features were striking, with high cheekbones, a slightly hooked nose, and wide, sensual mouth. Two deep lines ran from the sides of his nostrils to the corners of his lips, giving him a sardonic expression, and a black beard, streaked with silver, formed a sharp wedge on his chin.

He rose, carrying himself regally, his crimson caftan trimmed with ocelot and worn over a yellow satin tunic, the dagger in his sash studded with emeralds set in gold. A white egret adorned his turban, held in place by a cluster of diamonds.

Heather watched as he came nearer, till her head was level with his lower legs, encased in red leather boots with pointed, upward curling toes. He reached down and grasped her hand, lifting her up as he said, 'Rise, Pearl among Women. Tonight you shall be honoured above all others, when my organ of love gives forth its power, filling you with my seed.'

That voice! Dear God, it's like dark chocolate cream, she thought, lust racing through her from her tingling nipples to her needy clitoris. The aura of ruthless strength and authority, almost omnipotence, that emanated from him acted on her nervous system like a preparation made from cantharides.

'Where did you find her?' The Pasha questioned his servant, who had also fallen to his knees, face pressed against the tiles, enormous haunches quivering with fright.

'We took her when we raided the camp where the white men were excavating for relics, O Lord of my Existence!' he answered, his voice shaking. 'Is she not beautiful?'

'She is indeed, Fat One,' his master replied, eyes feeding on Heather, those brown beringed fingers holding hers loosely, his thumb pressing intimately into her palm.

'Thank you, Mighty Pasha,' the eunuch mumbled. 'May you live forever. Allah grant that the fruit of her womb will be sons.'

'Get up, Ugly Toad.' The pasha nudged him with his toe. 'You've served me well in this. I may reward you by permitting you to sodomise that lovely Greek youth who was recently delivered from the slave-market. He's a virgin, so I'm assured. If I discover that the trader was lying, then he'll be flogged! Not even I have enjoyed the boy yet. Open him for me – make him receptive. This is my command.'

The next time Heather came to herself, she was lying face-down on a padded couch, naked as the day she was born. So limp she could hardly move, she was aware of music in the background. It tinkled, piped, offered strange cadences that caressed the ear and added to her dreamlike state, intimate, mystical, with every note embroidered.

Now she could feel soft hands working on her, deft fingers massaging away every ache with the application of sweet scented oils – every ache, that is, save lust. Now delicate, now strong, the touch of those unseen hands roused even as they soothed.

Across her shoulder-blades they travelled, down her spine, dipping between the relaxed crease of her bottom, massaging the taut rosebud of her anus. It opened a smidgen at the delicate but insistent probing of a fingertip. Heather moaned her need, wriggling against that invading digit even though ashamed of the strange raw pleasure cascading through her loins.

'Hush, relax – enjoy—' whispered a gentle female voice.

Rectum, vagina, clitoris, all felt they were on fire – an unholy trinity of desire.

'Roll over, madam,' someone said persuasively.

Heather did as she was bidden, and the room swung into focus, not the anti-chamber in which she had met the Pasha, but another, smaller room, though equally exotic. Three women were attending her – beautiful girls, their sequinned boleros barely covering their opulent breasts and jutting nipples. Their spangled skirts were so sheer that it was easy to see their swelling mounds divided by hairless, alluring clefts.

The chief masseuse oiled her hands again. The nails were almond shaped, the palms hennaed in swirls and patterns. Heather gave a deep sigh as those hands resumed their magic. Starting at her throat, they crept over her naked body, sinking into every little fold – under her arms, circling her breasts, reaching up to smooth over the hungry peaks, gliding away. Heather moaned as those repeated sweeps roused her but did not satisfy.

Waves of feeling poured through her. She parted her legs and lifted her pubis in dire need. The girl smiled, her warm, cinnamon-spiced breath flicking across Heather's nipples. Her hand made practised movements on her victim's mons veneris without touching the tip of her clit, whose plump, oval head swelled wantonly from its fleshy pink cowl, desperate for contact.

Heart thudding, Heather wondered if she dare ask her to rub it, but just as she was about to speak—

'Time to attire yourself, madam. The Illustrious Lord will be here soon,' one of the other women said.

Frustrated, aching, love-juices smearing her thighs, Heather stood while the women started to braid her hair with ribbon and ropes of seed pearls. They were so lovely, so graceful, jewels of womanhood preparing a gift for the sultan's bed.

Still not quite sober, Xanthia's potion strong enough to last through the night, Heather wanted to caress them, to feel those heavy breasts in her hand, firm nipples grazing her palm, before dipping down to the smooth skin of their depilated quims. If only someone, she was beyond the point of caring who, would attend to the wants of her over-active clit.

A pier-glass, tilted on its stand, gave back her reflection in the subdued light. As she moved, she wafted the strong smell of sex mingled with that of roses, as if she had been steeped in their perfume for hours.

'Madam?' An open-fronted silk gauze chemise was slipped over her upper arms and shoulders, so fine that her nipples stood out against the fabric, dark and pointed. This was left open to the waist, the deep valley between her breasts clearly visible.

'Madam?' Another girl, slender as a boy, was holding out a pair of baggy pantaloons in leaf-green tiffany, brocaded with silver flowers.

Heather stepped into them and the girl kneeled to fasten the buttons at the ankle. Before she eased them over Heather's hips, however, she moved closer, looking up, eyebrows raised, as if asking permission. Heather nodded, breath rushing back into the cavity of her mouth in joyous anticipation. At last!

She could see the two other attendants standing behind her, one each side. The mirror threw back a clear, stimulating image as they reached round and began to stroke Heather's nipples. An ache, so strong as to be almost pain, radiated from those tormented crests. The girl kneeling before her gently parted Heather's dark-fringed labia, dipped a finger in the nectar seeping from her vulva, and massaged the hood

152

backwards and forwards over the eager clitoris till it stood out, pink, gleaming and proud.

Heather's head went back, her throat arched, the most delirious sensations holding her in thrall. She straightened, opened her eyes, looked at herself in the mirror, excitement mounting at the sight of the two girls busily engaged in pleasuring her breasts, and the dark head of the third on a level with her cleft. She opened her legs a little, making it easier for her female paramour, and the fingers massaging her bud were replaced by the exquisite feel of a tongue-tip.

Heather cried out plaintively. The tongue continued its artful lapping, the fingers holding back the labia firmly but gently. No one can know a woman's greatest means of arousal except another woman, Heather thought, while thought was still possible. It's the first time I've been sucked by female lips, but it won't be the last.

The madness was in her now, that insane drive towards orgasm which nothing must interrupt. Those fingers on her nipples sending shock waves down to her clit – the clit itself like an enormous bud ready to burst under the caresses of that deft, skilled and wickedly efficient pink tongue.

She was about to let herself be drawn into that wonderful stage when climax is inevitable when she suddenly looked beyond the mirror. There, on the terrace, outside the opened casement, stood a man – watching avidly.

She recognised him instantly. It was the Pasha, dressed in a flowing white robe. It was ruched up at the front and he was holding a truly impressive penis – short, thick and circumcised – in both hands. Hanging beneath this enormous prong were a pair of balls, large and mobile in their scrotal sac. Wielding it like a club, he rubbed his cock purposefully, little droplets flying from it as he watched the odalisques bringing Heather to orgasm.

It was too late for her to stop now. The sight of him masturbating as he watched her being pleasured was the last straw. She came in a welter of ecstasy so intense that it left her weak and gasping. She felt as if lava was gushing from her, hot and molten. While she was still convulsing, the Pasha gave a great shout and rushed towards her. Picking her up in his arms, he flung her down on the couch and straddled her, his engorged cock poised above her opening for a second before he thrust its turgid width into her with a force that made her yell.

'Don't cry out, beloved captive,' he muttered. 'Tonight you are my Chosen One—' and with a final spasm, he poured out his tribute.

For a moment, she was crushed beneath his solid body, then he took his weight on his elbows, smiling down at her, a hand either side of her face. 'How beautiful you are,' he said, in that cultured, mellow voice with its foreign intonations. 'It is time for us to bathe, my jewel – then I have other ways of love I wish to show you.'

He rose, clapped his hands, and the slave-girls bowed themselves out. Heather was alone with this Eastern potentate – his captive, so he said – his slave, too. She wasn't quite sure if she liked this idea, though there was no denying that such power was exciting. He was quite a lot older than her – in his early forties, and this, too, stirred her sexually.

The father/lover dichotomy. All masterful – all dominating. Wasn't there a corner in every woman's psyche that responded to this dark, forbidden, incestuous passion? Her husband, Charles, had been older than her, but weak when

154

it came to sex. The Pasha certainly was not!

She found herself unable to do other than obey this forceful, passionate man, and walked over the soft ochre and white carpet to a room given over entirely to luxury. No expense had been spared to produce a delightfully relaxing atmosphere, the hues lapis-lazuli, umber and terracotta. The oval bath, set into the tiled floor, was of pale green marble, veined in white. The water gushed from a shell-shaped fountain.

There were alcoves holding jars and bottles, and Heather removed the cut glass stoppers from one, then another, choosing oil to add to the warm tub. Having selected patchouli, she poured in a generous measure, then stepped down into it. She was not quite sure if she was awake or dreaming, and this feeling increased when the Pasha strode in looking harder, larger, somehow more menacing without his clothes. His hair, sprinkled with grey, was freed from the turban, and swept back into sepia curls.

His body was muscular, the shoulders wide, the chest deep, waist trim, his thighs and legs like firm pillars upholding that iron torso. Dominating all was his broad, stocky phallus, a stalwart weapon ever ready to answer the call.

Its skin was brown, embossed with veins like the roots of some gnarled tree, the bulging naked glans twin-lobed and glossy, robbed of its foreskin. As if a living creature quite independent of its owner, it thrust out belligerently from the black thicket of his underbelly, a shaft of flesh with a massive purple head. Once again it was at a ninety-degree angle, the fuck that had taken place earlier a mere aperitif, not the main course.

He stood, legs wide spread, on the tiled floor by the side of the tub, illumined by the glow from the gold and silver lamps which hung from the painted rafters. Heather, looking up, saw his hand move to his testicles, cradling their weight, fondling them gently. They were the balls of a mature man, and one dangled slightly lower than the other. No youthful plums these, but massive fruit hanging in a velvety net, ripe with the promise of luscious juice.

She waited for him in the water, heart pounding in her breasts, nipples tingling, her vagina aching to be pierced by his regal, tumescent spear.

He lowered himself into the tub, white teeth gleaming in a wide smile. Heather poured the warm, heavily-scented water over him, then soaped his body, lingering on the area between his legs, enjoying the spongy feel of his testicles, and that impudent cock which seemed to be everywhere at once. Wherever her hand went, there it appeared to push itself into her palm, demanding caresses.

The Pasha, a connoisseur of sensuality, lay there rumbling contentedly like a big tomcat, while she idled by his side, flicking perfumed drops from her fingertips over his chest and belly, watching in fascination as they trailed down to brush the knob of his upthrusting phallus. He closed his eyes and sighed deeply, relishing the delight of it.

'My new concubine,' he said in that deep voice, his sensitive, ringed fingers stroking her flesh. 'My Queen of the Night! If you please me, I may marry you, beloved.'

His hand was in her hair, still stroking, still caressing, and when he kissed her his tongue was as fat and wet as his penis, diving into her mouth insistently, licking the roof, her gums, entwining with her own darting organ of taste and touch. It was intoxicating, and the excitement raged more fiercely as his hand located her fringed lips under the water.

His fingers made slow, circular movements round the swelling head of her clitoris, caressing her with an experienced accuracy that brought her swiftly to the edge. Then he held off, smiling mischievously into her eyes and, hand in hers, lead her from the bath. She was weak and dizzy from the warmth and the wine, her disappointed bud aching for release. She hurt with desire, yearning to be taken by this powerful, handsome man.

The doors swung open and Heather glided over the threshold into his bed-chamber. For a moment it seemed that she looked into an orb of gold, then realised that it was a circle of light from a crystal lamp that hung near the divan. The Pasha guided her forwards, to the cloth-of-gold hangings that were looped back with massive fringed cords.

'Come, Moon of my Delight,' he murmured, and she found herself with him in his curtained bower. 'Let me suck your breasts and feast on the nectar from that perfumed garden between your thighs.'

Their bodies were damp from the bath, the air both cooling and regenerative. The Pasha's shaft had not relaxed, and it still held that shiny head high, bedewed with the clear fluid engendered by his arousal. Amused to act as her slave instead of vice versa, his hands shook a little as he took up a porcelain jar, removed the lid and annointed his palms with magnolia-scented unguent.

'Give yourself over to pleasure, beloved,' he crooned, his hands soft on her skin. 'You are like a young, delicate blossom waiting for the kiss of the sun to awaken to its full glory. The slave-women did this to you and I saw how you responded, your love-bud rejoicing at their touch. How much better it will be for you if I do it. Let me look at your treasure, that divine pearl which nestles so sweetly between your secret lips.'

The sensual curve of his bearded mouth more pronounced, he concentrated on her clitoris. He circled it, rubbed it, coaxing it to venture from its concealing hood. The blood gathering under the almost transparent membrane had rendered it rose-pink. It quivered desperately, over-loaded with impending pleasure.

With that streak of cruelty inherent in his nature, the Pasha laughed and withdrew his fingers, taking one of her nipples into his mouth. Having added to her torment until she was practically screaming, he said, his voice harsh with sexual need: 'You want it so very badly, don't you? Then beg for it.'

'Oh, please! Be merciful! I can't endure any longer!'

She was being subjected to his sexual will, seeing the hynotising lust reflected in his eyes, but she didn't care. All she wanted was rescue from where she was stranded, near the peak but unable to scale it without help. Her heart was pounding so hard with anticipation that she thought it would burst.

'Ask me again to make you come.' His tone was honeyed now, his fingers working relentlessly on her avid, puckered nipples.

'Please make me come,' she whimpered.

'You must say it properly. "Please, my lord, make me come."'

'Please, my lord, make me come,' she repeated parrot-fashion.

With well-judged skill, he suddenly reached down and rubbed the head of her clitoris with his forefinger. The orgasm was so powerful that she screamed with pleasure, spasms juddering through her, making her head reel and her body convulse.

'Wonderful woman,' he purred and, while the ripples were still undulating through her, he plunged his shaft into her dripping aperture, not coming, but giving her muscles something to clench around. Then he withdrew.

He controlled his passion, resisting the need to flood her with his seed, satisfied to feel her hand clasping his pulsating rod while he stimulated her further, bringing her to mini-climaxes, letting her rest for a few moments, then making her crave it again.

Finally he rolled her over in his arms and laid her on her stomach. He lay on top of her, his penis a hard ridge pressing against her spine, as he tied her wrists to the bedposts. Panting with excitement, he caressed her bottom with his hands and tongue, then raised her to her knees.

Heather clenched her buttocks. She guessed his intention and wasn't sure if she wanted penetration in the place where she was still a virgin. Her nostrils were the first organs to be seduced, the scent of jasmine and attar of roses, the ripe odour of juices – his and hers. The Pasha spread her buttocks wide and she felt warm oil trickling down the dark avenue between them. She could not help thrusting backwards towards his touch, opening herself to his desires, but gave a yelp when his finger penetrated her tight hole, her muscles resisting this strange invasion.

He ignored her reluctance, his finger entering to the first knuckle then the second, until finally the whole of it was buried in her warm, oily depths. He pulled out slightly and added two more, widening the opening.

His other hand was beneath her, craftily

caressing her mound, the lips stretched apart by her posture, the clitoris vulnerable and exposed, hanging down like a miniature penis. He pinched and tweaked it, rolled it between his forefinger and thumb, finding its very root. A violent orgasm shocked through her. While she was still moaning and gasping, she felt his rock-hard member pressing against her anal ring.

'Oh, no – don't,' she pleaded, but was denying the dark, dangerous tide within herself. She wanted him to explore this forbidden place, needed to know how it felt, curiosity and passion in full spate.

The smooth head of his phallus homed in on her slippery, puckered spincter and she cried out at this strange way of taking as he commenced to deflower her. He was too aroused to stop, pressing her face down into the pillow, his hand still cupping her mound, middle finger working on that insatiable clit which reared up for more.

She shivered at this new sensation as he pushed into her with fierce little thrusts, her moans of pleasure muffled by the satin cushions. Even as her bud sped onwards towards orgasm, so she could feel her body expanding, opening to take all of him, till his pubic hair brushed against her buttocks, his shaft buried deep inside her.

As she reached a thunderous climax so, with a frenzied burst of energy, the Pasha's prick jerked as he groaned in ecstasy, spurting into her.

'Sweetest jewel,' he murmured, withdrawing his briefly deflated tool. 'I may very well make you my wife. I have twelve already, but you shall be the latest and most beloved.'

Heather lay beside him without moving, feeling as if every tender, delicate membrane in her loins was on fire. Yet she had wanted it. Never a coward, she was willing to drain every experience

to the dregs but, for the moment, was un
satiated. There was a carafe of red wine by the
bedside and she drank a glassful, welcoming its
soporific effect. Needing nothing more now than
to sleep, she pulled the quilted coverlet over her
and curled into a ball.

Just before she drifted off, she heard the Pasha
say, 'You are mine now, and mine you will
remain, while life exists in your lovely body. I
demand complete and absolute fidelity. No
matter how much I adore you, my sweet, if I
discover that you've been unfaithful I shall order
you to be sewn up in a sack, weighted, and
thrown into the sea. This is how we deal with
adulterous wives.'

Chapter Nine

THE SKY WAS of a brilliant Italian blue. The high garden walls and tall sentinel trees screened the garden. A somnolent hush, broken only by occasional birdsong and the drone of bees extra busy over the fragrant thyme beds, brought to mind the tale of *Bluebeard's Castle*.

Lunch was served on the terrace – barbequed spare ribs still fizzing under a silver cover, wholemeal bread, a comb of heather-honey and a purple bunch of grapes were spread out invitingly. Bottles stood in mahogany coolers, with slender-stemmed wine-glasses alongside.

'Don't be deceived by the weather. The locals say there's thunder on the way,' Xanthia remarked, a scarlet sari wound round her body under her breasts, the colour complimenting the strawberry ripeness of her nipples and the golden glow of her skin.

It was her cardinal rule that, through the summer months, she never took part in anything until the sun went down. 'Cornwall can be capricious,' she continued, stabbing a glance at Heather. 'Sun and storms, fair or foul – copying life, really. Speaking of which, have you decided not to be a man's slave?'

'To be perfectly frank, I found certain aspects of the Pasha's domination rather exciting,' Heather admitted. She was wearing a bikini – more conventional than the one originally supplied by Xanthia, but brief nonetheless. The sensation of the cane seat pressing against her anus through the skimpy crotch was reminiscent of that Eastern potentate's rollicking attentions.

'You knew it was a game,' Xanthia temporised, slowly peeling a peach, as absorbed in this delicate task as if she was pushing back some fortunate lover's foreskin. 'Imagine if you really had been a prisoner in his seraglio. I think you'd have grown to hate it, and him. The harem women were – still are I guess – birds in a gilded cage, kept solely to boost one man's ego.'

'Tell me about it!' Julie butted in, burgeoning in all directions in a white crop-top and the tightest of denim shorts. 'That guy I was supposed to have been sold to – what a conceited prat! But d'you know what? It ended up that he wanted me to pee over him. That *was* exciting. I'd never done it before, and it was a helluva turn-on.'

'Watersports,' Xanthia murmured, peach liquid wetting her lips and trickling over her taste-buds.

'I thought that meant intercourse in the bath,' Heather interrupted, dismayed by her ignorance. There was so much yet to learn.

'No, dear, it's a term for urolagnia,' Xanthia explained patiently. 'Sometimes the man wants to do it over the woman, but it's more satisfactory for her if she's the donor.'

'It could simply be a regression to infancy,' André put in coolly.

He was on his third cup of coffee, lounging indolently at the table, devastatingly fuckable in a pair of gaudy Burmudas. His deeply tanned chest and back were exposed, a curl of black fuzz under

163

his armpits, the odour of *Jazz* so much more pleasant than sweat. He winked at Heather and reached for the grapes.

'Whatever the cause, and I don't think it's necessary to go into lengthy analysis, it's just another aspect of sex play,' Xanthia concluded. She leaned across and ran a caressing finger down Julie's deep cleavage. 'You're doing fine. No fear of *you* backsliding. But I'm not so sure about Heather. There's this tendency towards sentimentality and the doormat syndrome. It's worrying.'

André smiled sardonically. 'What's the lesson today, Teach?'

'You won't be here?' Xanthia asked with a frown. 'I miss you.'

He pushed back his chair and rose, and the sight of such a lithe, sexy beast made Julie writhe uncomfortably in her tight denim shorts. 'I'm busy. Pirates are due to land on the beach and there's the usual furore of duelling, rape and roistering. Our clients love it. There's nothing quite like a good old "yo-ho-ho and a bottle of rum". But it requires a lot of stage-managing so that everyone's satisfied – the buccaneers, the nautically-minded gays, and the women.'

'Can I come and watch?' Julie breathed, jumping up and going over to rub her breasts against his chest.

'If you watch you'll undoubtedly come,' he grinned, an arm round her. 'I'll give you a part, if you like. What d'you want to be? A captured lady, a wench or a pirate queen?'

'Don't forget the Regency romp tonight,' Xanthia reminded him, getting to her feet with feline grace, hips swaying beneath the loose covering as she shimmied towards the house.

Her boudoir was filled with the languid scents

of summer, the sunlight filtering through the shutters throwing golden bars across the highly-polished parquet. Heather, sleepy from the night's exertions and the excellence of the lunch-time wine, sank into the luxuriant depths of one of the couches.

Xanthia dropped her sari. No one could call her unselfconscious. She was extremely *conscious* of her body, glorying in its pleasures and power over others. Heather could not help staring at that beautiful flesh stretched so smoothly over the fine bones. Her narrow hips and slender waist added to the impression of aristocratic elegance. Xanthia smiled, moved closer.

'D'you want to touch me? Haven't had a woman yet, have you?' She took Heather's hands in her own and placed them on her breasts.

It was as if Heather held her own weighty boobs. Such satiny brown skin, so round and perfect in contour. And the nipples – larger, more satisfyingly sensitive than a man's. Because she knew how she felt when her own were rubbed it enabled Heather to pleasure Xanthia's. Slowly, hesitantly, she followed her mentor's urging and applied her lips to those puckered tips.

Joy, long-forgotten but now remembered, lit up her brain like a firework display. Had she been breast-fed or put on the bottle? She dimly recalled being told that her mother had made the ultimate sacrifice of time and figure by suckling her for the first few weeks of her life. Now, thrilling with a combination of contentment and sexual desire, Heather lapped Xanthia's rosy nipples.

'Good. You do that well,' Xanthia sighed, pushing aside Heather's bikini bra and fondling her breasts, too. 'Tell me, do you really love men more than women?'

'I don't know. Ask me later, when I've had

more experience.' Heather did not want to be drawn into conversation. She was living again that seering moment when the slave girl had knelt before her and licked her hungry bud to orgasm. She wanted to do the same to Xanthia.

'May I?' She dropped down before her, in a gesture of gratitude and submission.

She eased Xanthia's long legs apart, caressed the avenue between, and gently inserted a finger. It felt unusual, new, exciting, yet as familiar as when she touched herself. Xanthia sighed and closed her eyes, her arms hanging limply at her sides.

Heather kissed her belly, her navel, then moved the tip of her tongue towards Xanthia's cleft, narrow and smooth as a virgin's. Now, greatly daring, she moistened the edges of the protruding pink wings, licked inside them, then found Xanthia's clitoris. It hardened at once, increasing in size. She drew it into her mouth, stimulated it with little nibbles, wetted it with saliva, made it moved up and down.

Heather slipped her middle finger into her own vulva, spreading the juice over her crease and up to her clitoris. As she masturbated, she continued to tongue Xanthia. Her teacher's swollen nub and wet cleft felt so good, the fragrance similar to that of her own juices – not masculine and earthy, but more refined, with the salty tang of wave-washed shells.

Xanthia did not yield to climax. Her hands held Heather's face, easing her away. Then she went to an enormous carved oak chest, lifted the lid and drew out a casket. It was old, oblong, made of tooled leather inlaid with gold, about the size and shape of a vanity case. Carrying it carefully, she set it down on the divan. Turning the little key in the elaborate brass lock, she opened it.

There, against a red plush lining, was a collection of dildoes of all shapes, sizes and colours. Heather looked down at them in wonder. There were thick ones, thin ones, red ones, cream ones, vast black ones knotted with veins. Banana shaped, cucumber curved, some made of rubber which cloyed to the touch – others, obviously much older, carved out of cool ivory or polished wood.

All resembled phalluses, even the most modern of smoothly finished plastic, which, when Xanthia flicked a switch, buzzed like a horde of demented wasps.

'Which d'you want to try first?' she asked, sitting back on her heels, knees demurely together, only the very top of her crease revealed.

'I don't know. There're so many. I've not used one before.' Heather's fingers hovered over these treasures. 'You advise me.'

'All right. How about this dear little vibrator? It's the first one I ever owned. I was shy in those days, and had it delivered by mail-order.' Xanthia lifted it out, caressing its white, serrated sides and small curved tip. 'It's not the most impressive of my collection, but it will open your eyes, and your pussy, to a different sensation. Sit on the edge of the couch.'

Heather, heart thumping, did as her teacher said, spine upright, thighs open. The dildo hummed as Xanthia handed it to her, its vibrations travelling through her palm to her arm. Holding it in her right hand, she pushed aside the tiny triangle of material covering her mons and permitted the busy robot to make contact with the apex of her clitoris.

Pleasure shocked through her, so intense that she cried out. It was too much and, giving her bud a moment's respite, she stroked the vibrator down her furrow. It roved over the pink, wet surface, making the lips swell. Growing bolder, driven by an enormous wave of lust and needing to relieve it, she allowed it to touch her aching bud once again.

This was pure, unadulterated heaven. Never had she known such bliss. It was almost too much to bear – those continuous prickles rippling from the machine to her ultra-sensitive epicentre. It speeded up her reactions. What would have taken much rubbing to achieve happened almost instantaneously. Unable to control it, she came against the vibrating head with a force that bore her to euphoric heights she had never dreamed existed.

Stabbing the thing into her vulva, she clenched round it as the spasms continued to shock through her. Then, without pause, she applied it to her clitoris again, showing that ardent organ no mercy. It swelled and tingled and jerked as she applied hard pressure with the dildo. Orgasmic waves began to lave her once more – toes, legs, thighs, loins – until she exploded into another mighty convulsion.

'You've found your perfect pleasure tool,' Xanthia remarked, bending over her and watching. She stroked Heather's hair from her damp brow and kissed her eyelids, seeing how soft, relaxed and childlike was her expression. 'It may not look much like a penis – too small you might thing – but what a wizard.'

'It's amazing. I want to go on and on,' Heather breathed, lying back and refusing to remove it from her greedy, sensation-seeking pussy.

'So you can. I've climaxed a dozen times on the trot with that little darling,' Xanthia answered enthusiastically. 'Satisfaction's guaranteed. One's in absolute control, unlike when sharing sex with another person. It's like masturbation – perfect pleasure for oneself alone, but with an added kick. You can borrow it any time you want, but remember to put it back in the box. There're plenty of batteries if you burn those out.'

Left to herself while Xanthia returned to sun-worship, Heather spent the most sexually gratifying afternoon of her life. The simplicity of it was a revelation. Why didn't every woman own a vibrator? she wondered, as it darted and played around her lustful pudenda. Who, in reality, needed the complications inherent in a sex motivated relationship when such an obliging companion existed? Cheap to purchase, economical to run, always there. It would never argue, cheat or let one down. Heather was utterly converted as she reached yet another orgasm induced with a little help from her humming friend.

Yet, as the sunlight moved across the room and that sweet, magical time of twilight approached, she began to muse on men. Laying the vibrator aside, she allowed her mind to fill up with visions of handsome heroes. The dildo satisfied her physically, far more easily than any man, but what about the emotions?

Xanthia dismissed these, suspicious of entanglement, and her attitudes and way of life offered hedonistic sexual liberation. But Heather still sat on the fence, not entirely convinced. Whilst the vibrator was arousing her to those extraordinary peaks she wanted nothing else. But when she allowed the beauty of the evening to penetrate her soul, then the urge for romantic love swept through her again.

It's women's minds and hearts that are their worst enemies, she sighed, the feminine need for something other than bodily pleasure.

The soirée was in full swing when Heather arrived in the reception room that night. Xanthia held court there, reclining on a scroll-backed Directoire couch. Her costume was of the early 1800s, and her white high-waisted, semi-transparent gown, her up-swept hair and black ballet-pumps aped the style of Josephine, Napoleon Bonaparte's consort. The deliberately dampened single lawn garment worn beneath clung shamelessly to every curve and hollow.

André sat beside her, slouched low on his spine, one arm extended along the back. He, too, was attired in clothes of the period, cutting a dash as a dandy. It suited his tall, lean figure: the beige breeches, so tight that it looked as if he had been poured into them, showing off his bulge remarkably well, and ending in shiny black riding boots.

His cravat and collar were very large, and his gentian-violet jacket had excessive revers. It was short-waisted in front and had tails at the back. His hair had been brushed forward in that casual style called the 'Brutus' cut, and he rose to make an elegant leg to Heather as she came towards them.

'Stap me, André, and who is this ravishing creature?' asked a man who was leaning over Xanthia, one of his fingers trailing negligently along the top of the apology for a bodice that barely covered her nipples.

'My cousin, Miss Heather, but newly arrived from Bath, Lord George,' André answered, presenting her.

Heather dipped into a curtsey, aware that she looked girlishly appealing in a rose-pink gown girded by a sash of deeper red tied just beneath her breasts. They swelled above the low neckline, the gown as revealing as a nightdress. The bodice had minute puff sleeves, and the skirt was fuller behind, gathered into tiny pleats and falling into a small train. A velvet bandeau with a single pink ostrich feather bound her hair. She wore no underwear, and had thonged sandals on her naked feet.

George was of middle height and slightly built. His hair was shaggy and so fair that it suggested long exposure to the bleaching rays of a hot, foreign sun. He was dressed in the last extreme of fashion, with gold fobs dangling from his waistcoat. He lifted his lorgnette and quizzed Heather through it as they were introduced. Then he drew out a silver snuff-box and offered it to André.

Both men balanced a tiny dune on the base of their thumbs and sniffed delicately, before dabbing their nostrils with lace-edged handker-chiefs. How civilised, Heather thought, but they weren't, of course. Beneath those courtly man-ners and stylish costumes, most Regency rakes were vicious profligates.

'Will you honour me with a dance, Miss Heather?' George was close to her now, staring into her bodice. She could see the long line of his dick pressed against his inner left thigh under those exceedingly tight breeches.

'Thank you, sir,' she said, and rested the tips of her gloved fingers on the back of his outstretched hand.

The salon was ablaze with candles, the orchestra tuning up to play a gavotte. Heads turned when Heather and George took their places. Ladies whispered behind their fans and gentlemen glanced sideways at her. Everyone was turned out in the correct clothes and Heather admired Xanthia's skill in bringing to life any particular era in which she had decided her guests might enjoy themselves.

Heather peered up at George as they postured and twirled to the measure, fingertips touching. And what was her role tonight? Innocent maiden about to be debauched by a lecherous member of the *ton*? Shady lady from among the *demi-monde* intent on outraging society?

There was something disturbing about George's ice-blue eyes. She found that she could not read them as the set pattern of the gavotte brought them close together, her breasts brushing his chest, hands clasped firmly, the high ridge of his prick touching her thigh. He had a narrow, beautiful face, a thin supercilious nose, light brown lashes, and pointed brows over which tumbled that white-blond hair.

'Miss Heather, you seem a gal of rare spirit,' he said, as the dance finished but he remained standing with his arm about her, cock lifted now, outlined by those snug buckskins. 'I'd like you to meet some friends of mine. Corinthians to a man! Real out-and-outers! Patrons of the turf and the fancy. Come along, m'dear.'

Could she trust him? There was something about him which carried with it a whiff of dark alleyways and deceitful dealings. Yet he was pretty – almost too pretty, perhaps. Comforting herself by recalling that this was not real life but a charade invented by those accomplished tricksters, Xanthia and André, she went along with his suggestion.

He held her hand carefully as if it was a present he was not yet allowed to unwrap, and took her into a side-room where he introduced her to his friends, a raffish crowd by all accounts who were drinking, playing faro, and talking very loud and lewd.

Heather became a heroine from a Georgette Heyer novel. She drank too much champagne, giggled and flirted and aired her wit, telling herself that this was a truly fabulous age into which she had been catapulted. The Georgians had certainly known how to enjoy themselves, before stuffy Queen Victoria came to the throne and spoiled everyone's fun.

There were several other women in their party, half-naked, brazenly painted creatures, introduced as Cypriots – prostitutes in Regency parlance. Everything became hazy and Heather found herself enthroned on a couch with George. His hand was in her bodice and the flap of his breeches undone, displaying a penis which was quite out of proportion with his slim, girlish build. One of the women was on her knees in front of him, tongue and lips slurping at that huge, engorged member.

Beyond this point Heather's recollections became fragmentary, though she did recall George eating some ice-cream out of her hand and then licking every finger and even the palm with an air of thoughtless enjoyment. It struck her as rather unpleasant, even though she wished it was her clit he sucked.

Another dandy had taken possession of her breasts. He was drunk but kept it together, resplendent in coat of lavender brocade, with striped stockings and chisel-toed pumps.

Despite this finery, his aspect was alarming, for he had a scar down the left side of his face. 'It's an old sword-wound,' he explained, as he stimulated her nipples in the same detached manner as George when he licked her fingers. 'I got it duelling.'

'Don't listen to him, sweetheart,' George cut in, using that drawling, sarcastic tone they all affected. 'Harry's a notorious liar. He scagged his cheek when climbing down a drainpipe, running away from an irate husband who'd unexpectedly returned and found him rogering his wife!'

They danced. Heather lost a sandal somewhere and everyone crawled around searching for it. It was never found, so George and Harry made a chair of their arms and carried her out into the night where a carriage awaited.

Xanthia's weather forecast proved to be correct. The storm that had built up, latent and threatening, during the afternoon, broke overhead. A rumble of thunder rent the air. Violent forks of lightning split the black clouds apart and sent furious, drenching rain pouring down.

The sudden chill sobered Heather. She struggled from the arms that held her, but George caught her by the wrist, jerking it hard. Then, suddenly, Harry slipped a blindfold over her eyes, and that was when she wanted the game to stop.

'Take it off!' she shouted, unable to raise her arms. They, too, had been seized and tied.

She could feel hands all over her, and didn't know whose. She guessed that George was there, but without sight or touch could do nothing but submit to whatever he or his companions cared to do. There was a covert thrill in this, no matter how she ranted and raved. They would do with her as they wished and she would be absolved from blame.

The coach rolled into motion, swaying and jouncing. Heather tried to relax, but her head was swimming behind the blindfold. Too many champagne bubbles frothed in her brain, and whoever it was handling her flesh with such intimacy certainly knew her pleasure point. He (or maybe she) was concentrating on her clitoris.

Heather moaned, pressed upwards towards those unknown fingers, only to have them sharply withdrawn.

The coach halted and she stumbled down, guided by a hand under her arm. A high wind, the noisy storm, hushed but excited voices, slippery steps under the flimsy sole of her remaining sandal. She was descending, and it was colder now and damp, with a mouldy underground smell. There was the sound of water trickling – and every sound echoed.

No longer descending, her feet encountered firm rock. George whipped the scarf from her eyes and the bonds from her wrists. Heather blinked in the dazzle thrown by flares set in wall-sconces. She was standing in the centre of a large cave, a sinister place of deep shadows, lichen-covered walls and Gothic gloom. The seemingly endless roof disappeared into Stygian darkness.

Black candles in massive holders had been set at the four corners of a basalt altar. Their light danced over the bizarre paintings covering the wall behind it. These favoured the Satanic – obscene demons flourishing grotesquely large penises, winged beasts and centaurs penetrating the orifices of chained, nude figures of both sexes. Vampires, ghouls – blood, darkness – blasphemy.

Heather, chafing her bruised wrists, almost smiled. This was decidedly tacky. Surely Xanthia could have done better than reproduce the headquarters of the Hellfire Club? Heather had read about this brainchild of the decadent devil-worshipper, Francis Dashwood. Two hundred years ago he had got his kicks by holding orgies in the grotto of his family seat.

But mock it though she might, fear danced along her nerves. Those who had brought her there were drunk or high on other drugs. The illusion in the salon had been convincingly real. By now, George and Harry probably believed they were jaded Regency bucks in whom mysticism, spiritual frustration and religious guilt were at war and who needed weird and dangerous outlets.

And where do I feature in this? She wondered uneasily. Xanthia wouldn't let me be hurt, would she? *Or would she*?

Her apprehension deepened as those around stripped off their clothes and donned monks's habits, pulling the hoods up over their heads, men and women alike rendered impersonal, though their sex was clearly revealed through the opened fronts of the brown robes. They lined up on either side of Heather and then a stranger appeared from behind the altar. He, too, was robed, his face shadowed by a cowl. The others accorded him the reverence reserved for a priest.

'Hail, Master!' They chorused. There were a lot of people there, emerging from the darkness, all gowned and hooded.

'Strip her,' he commanded, his deep voice reverberating round the cavern.

Heather was riven with fear, yet at the same time had a vision of him tying her down and licking her slowly, his thick wet tongue worming its way into every pink furl and crevice. He reminded her of the doctor to whom she would be eternally grateful for introducing her to her clitoris and all its delights. She experienced a rekindling of lust, a wanton wetness seeping between her legs.

Two of the acolytes undressed her, after which she was conducted to the altar. Candle smoke drifted between herself and the faceless, hooded man who stood there, arms outstretched. Silence entombed them. Even the thunder could not penetrate that deep, dark underworld.

'What have you been doing, my child?' he questioned, his voice stern.

'Nothing,' she quavered, trembling with cold and fright.

'You must call me Master. Now, I repeat – what have you been doing?'

'Nothing, Master.'

'You lie. It is a sin to lie. You've been masturbating, haven't you? Caressing your private parts, giving yourself pleasure.'

'No, Master,' she mumbled, her cheeks burning with shame, but at the same time her vagina tightened and her clit swelled.

'Liars need to be punished, don't they, child?'

'Yes, Master.'

'So do naughty little girls who can't leave their pussies alone.'

'Yes, Master.'

'Let the punishment begin!' he shouted.

She was held steady while a hooded someone, she guessed it to be female, dipped slender hands into a bowl of fragrant oil and coated her breasts. With deliberate slowness, fingers flicked over the nipples, while, from behind her, Heather could feel other hands caressing her back and buttocks. She remained perfectly still and upright, thinking cunningly, if I behave and do exactly as I'm told, then maybe one of them will bring me to the climax for which I'm in such dire need.

Suddenly her arms were pinioned behind her back and handcuffs clicked on them. She jerked, cried out, her jutting pubis seized in a waiting hand. It was imprisoned, the labia pinched together, a finger teasing the inner flesh.

'Oow – oh – !' Heather shouted.

It was like an electric shock. She moved her

hips invitingly, but the finger did not do what she wanted. Only those others kept up their steady torment on her nipples, but there was to be no ease for her clitoris, not yet – not for a long time – maybe never. It was all down to the Master. His devotees would obey his commands.

She was aware of the pressure of a man's body at her back, felt a large cock pushing between her buttocks. Was it George's? And was it Harry's hands that fondled her parted thighs? She responded by rolling her hips, hoping the unknown dick would find her and enter her. It moved away, leaving her empty, sobbing with frustration. The finger on her mound was light, feathery, tantalising, making her gasp for more.

'Caress me there,' she begged. 'Caress me, please!'

'You must wait,' answered the Master from his position near the altar. 'Wait and watch.'

She was aware of movements in the dimness. Everywhere she looked hooded figures were coupling, in twos or threes – men and women locked into tangled groups. The cave was redolent of sex. It seemed to be coming at Heather from all directions, seeping through the greenish walls.

She was shaking, her bound hands burning to grasp an erect phallus. Slave to her desires, she yearned to give pleasure in the hope that the favour might be returned.

The Master was standing before her, and his hand shot out from the hanging sleeve, fastening on her mons – the other toying with her nipples. She desperately wanted to climax, but though he massaged her clit and fondled her breasts in the most experienced and tormenting way, taking her to the heights of enjoyment, just when she thought she was about to spill over, the touch was removed and her orgasm faded.

Urging her to her knees before him, he thrust his cock into her mouth. It was huge, but she obediently sucked on the pink dome, circling the crimson ridge. George took possession of her nether regions without ceremony, dipping into both openings alternatively. He kept thrusting into her, and Heather, squirming, shaking, tonguing the Master's penis, was enjoying it, never wanting it to stop. But still there was no climax for her.

The Master withdrew without coming, as much in command of himself as he was of his followers. Unseen hands unlocked the shackles and Heather was helped to her feet. She submitted to the blindfold again and felt herself being guided, lifted and bent over a firm object. It felt like a trestle, hard but not uncomfortable, padded in leather. She was spread-eagled, her arms and ankles tied, bottom raised.

It was not unpleasant, and she began to warm to this new game, so vulnerable, so open to all eyes. Anyone who wanted could touch her secret places and, as she hung there, they did. Soft touches, lips, fingers, no one hurt her and she took heart. If this was all part of Xanthia's lesson, then she would do her best to reap the benefit.

A slippery object, hard but not human, was slipped into her vagina, pushed backwards and forwards, bringing her intense pleasure and a further trickle of juices. To let her anonymous lovers know that she liked this, she threshed and moaned. A hand dived between her opened legs and touched her protruding lips, reaching the power point of her clitoris. A finger pressed on it, falling into that magical rhythm which brought her closer and closer and closer—

Then, utterly without warning, she felt a rush of air, heard a whistling hiss, and experienced shattering pain as a lash struck her bare bottom. She gave a yelp. Hands quickly stroked the mark. The whip came down again, and all the while that finger continued to excite her bud, enticing it, rubbing it, till, with the third kiss of the lash, she climaxed in a groaning, pleading tumult of desire, pain and pleasure.

Still spread-legged, she felt a penis push into her vagina, and a man's hard arms holding her. Bewildered, blind, tossed on a sea of confusing sensations, Heather relaxed and let him have his will of her, feeling his shuddering convulsions and the hot spurt of his come.

He lifted himself away from her, untied her bonds, took her tenderly in his arms and held her against the roughness of his habit as he freed her eyes. His followers were indulging in every sexual variation, and the smack of whips against bare flesh made her own body quiver in response.

'André,' she whispered, staring up groggily at him. 'You're the Master? The leader of this Satanic club? Why did you punish me?'

He smiled down at her, hood thrust back from his dark hair. 'It was part of the course. Another aspect of pleasure is fear, shame and pain. Haven't you sometimes thought of me as your confessor?'

'How did you know?'

'I guessed.'

He carefully laid her on the altar, rolled her on to her stomach and applied a soothing salve to the red wealds scoring her tender skin. Then, equally gently, he caressed her breasts, her face, her hair, and, wrapping her in an embroidered robe, carried her from the grotto by way of a secret passage that connected with Tostavyn Grange.

Chapter Ten

'*YOU SURE DO* look a picture, Missy Blanche. I done never seen a prettier bride. Mr Brad, he sure is a lucky man and no mistake,' enthused the portly, black, middle-aged woman as she stood back to admire Heather.

'Oh, hush your mouth, Mammy! You do go on so,' Heather breathed in that lisping, drawly voice used by Southern belles in costume movies like *Gone With The Wind* and *Jezebel*. Though in reality she'd not yet met him, she added, 'Mr Brad's a fine figure of a man.'

'That he is, Missy Blanche. But handsome is as handsome does, I always says, and he done got hisself a bad, bad reputation for gambling, and going around with women who calls themselves ladies but ain't no ladies, no sir!' Mammy grumbled, that privileged servant who had once been a slave. With a disapproving expression on her ebony face, she shifted her bulk about the elaborate state-room of the Mississippi paddleboat.

It was here that Blanche, nee O'Leary (she was Mrs Carforth, widow, but this had made so little impression on all and sundry that she was still known by her maiden name) of Seven Oaks plantation, and Brad Johnson, confederate officer, gun-runner and adventurer, were to spend the first night of their honeymoon.

'I want more romance!' Heather had declared, walking unannounced into Xanthia's bedroom on the morning after the Regency orgy. 'I accept that it was necessary for me to experience being kidnapped and whipped by debauched members of the Hellfire Club, but I was hoping for something more along the lines of that episode with Jake.'

Though Xanthia had been busy fornicating with both André and Jason, she had given Heather her solemn promise that the next scene should be in high Technicolor and very romantic.

'What would you like?' she had asked lazily, on her back beneath Jason who was kneeling over her, pumping in and out of her while André mounted him from the rear. 'The Deep South? Belles and beaux?'

'Yes, please,' Heather had answered promptly, amused to see that the three of them had resembled an erotic carving from an Indian temple. Sex, sex and more sex, any which way.

When evening came she had found herself on board a steamship. Her Fairy Godmother had once again waved her magic wand and conjured a perfect setting for Heather's fantasy. The brief had been as follows:

'OK. So you want to be a kind of Scarlett O'Hara. Here goes: You've just been married to a guy that's been after you for ages. You've lost all your money and property through the Civil War. You've accepted Brad because he's rich, denying that you really fancy him rotten. The guy I've selected for you is sweet, sweet flesh. It's your wedding night. Go for it. Make like your Auntie Xanthia – just in it for the endorphin rush! Do try to forget that brain aberration – love! It's fire and flame for a year – ashes for thirty!'

Now Heather glimpsed herself in the cheval mirror and grinned. Those mid-nineteenth century fashions were luscious. It had taken her a while to cope with the huge crinoline skirt, and her waist was laced so tightly that breathing was an effort till she got used to the whale-boning. Big, full sleeves, a low neckline, the gown a triumph of beige taffeta and cream lace. A wedding-gown, not white as she was supposed to have been married once already. A feathered, forward tilting toque surmounted her ringlets, and when she moved, she could feel the swish of the many petticoats that covered the hoop.

This was a decorous age, the wired skirts dictating that long drawers be worn beneath them. If not, every time the wind blew or the crinoline rode up, plump thighs and downy mounds would be on display. Heather's were fixed firmly in place, no open gussets this time, and reaching to below her knees where they ended in frills.

'Where is Mr Brad?' she exclaimed impatiently, getting into her role, flicking open her fan and pacing the luxuriously appointed cabin.

'He done told me he was going to the smoking saloon, Missy Blanche,' Mammy said, Creole hoops glinting, crinkly hair hidden beneath a white bandana. She cast a worried eye at her mistress.

'The gentlemen meet to play cards there, don't they?' Heather pouted, staring from the window.

It was dark outside, but she could see the shoreline drifting past, the stateroom vibrating to the chug-chug of revolving paddle-wheels. Music came from somewhere in this mock, three-tiered floating palace, with its gingerbread scrolling and twin stacks. It was most convincing, even though she knew that the passing scene of a river bank complete with oaks draped in Spanish moss was nothing more than a film-clip of night in Louisiana. It was that which moved, not the boat.

'They sure do, Missy,' Mammy commented. 'But it ain't fitting that you disturb him.'

'Fiddle-de-dee! I'm going to find him!' Heather announced, and floated towards the door, skirts dipping and swaying.

'I don't think you should do that,' Mammy objected, rolling her eyes. 'Genteel young ladies don't go into smoking-rooms, and you know it!'

'When will you learn that I'm not a genteel young lady, Mammy?' Heather retorted as she manoeuvred her crinoline over the threshold.

'Well, it ain't no blame to me,' Mammy scolded. 'I done my best for you, child, but you've been a wilful hussy since the moment that you was born when they laid you, bare-naked, in my arms.'

'Stop fretting about me so!' Heather said over her shoulder.

She was in a ferment to see whoever it was that was acting as Brad Johnson. If he came up to her expectations as a sort of Clark Gable lookalike, then she couldn't wait to share the nuptial couch with him.

The staterooms lined the sides of the great saloon, which was as long as two ballrooms placed end to end. It was tremendously ornate. White-painted iron pillars supported the vaulted ceiling. There were brass fittings, plush chairs, cut-glass oil lamps, bars and a restaurant, everything provided for the comfort of the well-heeled passengers travelling the mighty waterway.

A band played at one end, and the people occupying the little marble-topped tables and

velvet covered banquettes where superbly cos-
tumed in period gear – crinolines, bonnets, fans
and exotic shawls, morning suits, linen suits,
tartan trousers, silver-topped canes and tall silk
hats.

Heather wondered whether they, too, were
acting out their fantasies. Was she simply an extra
in some scenario of their own, as they were in
hers? Was this how Xanthia succeeded in keeping
everyone entertained?

Heather wandered the length of the saloon,
aware that she was attracting attention. Then she
came to a door with a coloured glass panel on
which the words 'Smoking Room. Men only'
were etched in gold lettering. She pushed it open
and sashayed in.

The air was blue, the space occupied by
baize-covered tables at which were seated a
number of flashily dressed gentlemen. No one
glanced up as she entered, each intent on the
game. Then, suddenly, she found herself meeting
a pair of bold green eyes that regarded her
quizzically.

'Can't you read, my dear?' The owner of these
impudent eyes asked loudly. 'It says "Men
only".'

He laid down his cards, pushed back his chair
and got to his feet, as did every one there. No
gentleman worth his salt ever remained seated
while a lady was standing, unless, of course, she
was a servant.

'Oh, mercy me! Does it?' she gasped, simpering
at the other men who were looking on with
interest, smiling indulgently, a fine collection of
traditional Mississippi gamblers. 'I declare, you'll
think me a silly goose! But I wondered where you
were.'

'It's flattering that you're so impatient for my

company,' he answered, subjecting her to a charming smile, though there was something guarded in his expression.

That's the understatement of the year, Heather thought, as she met the full force of his almost flagrant masculinity. Wow! she breathed inwardly. Will you look at that?

Not quite Clark Gable – a taller, slimmer version. Around thirty, he had dark hair that glinted with chestnut lights, a lean, sardonic face pierced by those sexy green eyes, and a thin line of dark moustache on his mockingly curled upper lip. As for his body? She could only guess at the magnificent proportions hidden by an immaculate dove-grey suit, frilled shirt, brocade waistcoat and paisley patterned cravat with a diamond pin.

If the other gamblers veered towards the tawdry, he was the perfect Southern gentleman. Superbly tailored clothes, gold cuff-links, a gold watch-chain, each item tasteful and ferociously expensive.

One of the men stepped closer to her, a dandy with peat-brown eyes and raven hair. He was wearing a burgundy velvet jacket, a canary yellow waistcoat and checked trousers, cut very tight, his bulge high and pronounced. He looked her over speculatively, one eyebrow arched, and then said in a French accent, 'You're welcome here, *mam'zelle*. Who are you? Johnson's doxy or a river-boat whore?'

Brad stiffened, his voice cool and steady as he butted in, 'Your attitude is insulting, *monsieur*.'

The dandy laughed unpleasantly, continuing to ogle Heather. 'Insulting? How can one insult such as she, sir? She's obviously come here in search of custom.'

'The lady is with me,' Brad said coldly, breeding showing in every angle of his face. He

186

placed a protective arm round Heather. 'Come along, my dear. This is no place for you. Neither is this *gentleman* suitable company.' He laid sarcastic emphasis on the word.

The Frenchman flushed, and a muscle quivered in his cheek. 'Take back that remark!' he hissed. 'Or else I may be forced to challenge you to a duel.'

'Any time,' Brad's tone was clipped and quietly threatening. 'Choose your weapons. Pistol or rapier. But you'll be a fool if you do, for I'm an expert at both.'

'You refuse to offer me an apology?' The Frenchman was fairly hopping with rage.

'I do, sir.'

'Then my seconds will call on you when we reach New Orleans.'

Brad looked him up and down, slowly, contemptuously, then he said, 'Really? I think it's you who should be apologising.' And he drew Heather forward, adding, 'May I present my wife? This is Mrs Johnson. We have only been married a few hours.'

The Frenchman gasped. '*Madame*, a thousand pardons!' he exclaimed, totally flustered. 'I had no idea. Forgive me.'

Poor boy, she thought, for he was very good-looking and that harsh husband of hers had been so scathing, but how wonderfully quick to defend her honour. It thrilled her to the marrow and she longed to be alone with him, hard and ruthless though he might be. The very fact that he was such a dominating man added to her excitement, causing her nipples to tingle beneath her chemise.

'I accept your apology, *monsieur*,' she replied graciously, and the Frenchman bowed, took her hand in his and raised it to his lips, while Brad looked on sardonically.

Then, 'You'll have to excuse me,' he said curtly

to the other gamblers, and carelessly tossed a wad of dollar bills on to the table among the playing cards and chips. 'I hope we may continue our game tomorrow.'

They nodded, so did he, and he took Heather's arm in his firm tanned fingers, guiding her from the smoking-room. At once any pleasantness vanished from his face. 'What the devil d'you mean by following me? It's no place for a lady,' he growled. 'I might have had to kill that young whelp because of your foolishness!'

'A duel, d'you mean? You could have refused!' she returned, head high, heart thumping at his nearness.

'I'm a gentleman. If a challenge is issued, then I can't back out of it. You'd have had the lad's blood on your conscience for behaving in such an irresponsible fashion.'

Heather was taken aback, but plunged recklessly into her part of the proud, high-spirited belle. 'Don't try lording it over me, sir!' she retorted. 'It's your fault. That's no way to treat your bride, leaving her alone while you gamble the night away with a gang of roustabouts!'

Brad grinned, anger disappearing, to be replaced by a look of such torrid desire that her knees turned to jelly. He pulled her closer in the shelter of a pillar, and his mouth swooped on hers. He kissed her thoroughly and with great expertise – the edge of her lips, the yielding softness beyond, his tongue dipping in, touching the tip of hers.

Heather could feel herself ripening, softening, wanting only to be devoured. His long legs were pressed hard to hers and, even with the restrictions imposed by her censuring hoop and his narrow trousers, she was aware of the hardness of his sex moving against her.

188

'Let's go to bed,' he whispered, his moustache tickling her neck as he bent to kiss it. 'I've waited years for this, ever since I first saw you running barefoot through your father's cotton fields. You were a chit of twelve and I swore then that one day I'd fuck you.'

'Mr Johnson! Such language!' She pretended to be outraged, but inside she was lusting after him like no other.

He pulled a suitably contrite face, and said sarcastically, 'My deepest apologies, Mrs Johnson.'

Then he marched her briskly through the saloon and into their stateroom. It was empty. 'Where's Mammy?' Heather asked immediately.

'I gave her the evening off, and plenty of money to spend enjoying herself. This night is ours – long and uninterrupted, a night in which I'm going to show you just how much I love you.' His voice was low and husky, his drawl genuine, a dyed-in-the-wool American. 'I could spend two weeks between silken sheets with you, Blanche. I want to know every inch of you, inside as well as out. You're a spoilt, exasperating, delicious little bitch. You've tormented me long enough. All those other beaux you've encouraged – pretending that you hated me.'

'You must give me time, sir.' Heather tried to pull away, though her breasts were arching towards him, clitoris throbbing. 'I need Mammy to undress me.'

'Don't play coy!' he snapped, deft fingers beginning to undo the row of pearl buttons that fastened the back of her bodice. 'You don't need anyone but me to do it. Goddammit! You're no virgin. You were married to Edward Carforth, weren't you?'

'We had one night together and then he

marched off to war and was killed. He was only a boy. He'd never done it before. Neither had I. It hurt, and I thought – well, if this is what the great secret's all about then it's hugely overrated.' Heather allowed him to turn her around so that he could manage the buttons better.

'Poor little girl,' he chuckled, brushing his lips along the nape of her bare neck while his hands completed their task and her dress rippled down to puddle at her feet. 'So, he didn't make you come, eh? You know what I'm talking about, don't you? I'll bet you've played with yourself.'

He was behind her, pressing close. His hands came round to push down the lacy chemise and cup her breasts that jutted above her corset. Those knowing fingers gently pinched the hardened nipples, and she arched her spine, unable to resist wriggling her bottom against the upraised tribute of his hunger-stiffened phallus.

She checked herself. She mustn't seem too wanton. Her role was that of a sensual woman who has never been fulfilled by a man. She couldn't yet give in to the frantic desire to offer him her backside like a bitch on heat.

'I don't know what you're talking about,' she managed to gasp.

She could feel the laughter rumbling up through his deep chest, and he swung her round so that she could not avoid his tantalising mouth and smiling, sea-green eyes. 'Actions speak louder than words. I'm going to teach you, honey,' he promised in that sultry, dark-brown voice.

She glanced down at his hands which had begun to work on the lacing of her stays. Beautiful hands, sensitive and strong. The hands of a lover, hands which had known the bodies of many women. She wanted to feel his fingers fondling the hard, wet bud of her clitoris.

190

This was so much more to her taste – the lush Hollywood trappings, the big brass bed with nets hanging from a centre coronet, the pink-shaded lamps, the crimsons and gold-leaf, and this magnificent man who embodied her every dream of the romantic hero.

Once her body was free to his gaze, naked save for the cream silk stockings upheld by lacy garters, wordlessly he lifted and carried her to the bed. Then he took her face between his hands and drew it up towards his mouth. His lips touched hers, teased them, opened them, the faint smell of Havana cigars on his breath, mingled with whisky. It was pleasant, warm, reminiscent of Christmas, of pine cones and holly and cosy fires, and she lay in his arms like a trusting child.

'You're so lovely,' he breathed, and kissed her again as if he was starving, the heat of passion radiating from him.

'D'you really mean that? I'll bet you say that to all the girls,' she dimpled at him, though it was hard to keep up the pretence of flirtation when she was craving satisfaction.

He looked down at her, eyes serious. 'I mean it, Blanche. I want to pet you, pamper you, give you all the things that the war took away. When we dock in New Orleans I'll take you on a shopping spree.'

He left her and proceeded to strip rapidly, flesh glowing in the lamp-light. First his jacket was hung on the back of the chair, followed by the cravat and waistcoat, then the white shirt. He sat down to ease off his highly polished shoes and black silk socks. Everything about him was immaculate and uncreased, a fastidious man used to the services of a valet, though perfectly capable of self-sufficiency if circumstances demanded.

He returned to the bedside, wearing only his

close-fitting trousers that emphasised those well-muscled thighs and the heavy bulge of his penis. Heather could not resist slipping a hand into the fly. His prick was iron-hard, and its hot, silky length fitted into the groove of her palm. He made a small noise deep in his throat, dropped his pants and stood naked before her.

Heather's vulva spasmed, the sight of him enough to addle a saint's brain and bring a nun to climax. A tanned, muscular torso, dark hair furring his chest and scrawling down past his navel to gather round his genitals. His cock sprang forth from its bush, long and upward-pointing, and the balls that hung beneath it were large and full and mature, swinging in their downy sac.

He sank down on the bed beside her, and she found his shaft again, rubbing it firmly, rejoicing in his response, while he pressed his tongue inside her ear, his fingers petting her nipples. She shivered with the compelling combination of tongue and hand. She was mad for him, writhing against him, forgetting that she was supposed to be an unschooled young widow who had never before known sexual completion. This was the one! She knew it!

All the scenes she had been through till now were as nothing. She wanted this man to be hers for all time – to sleep with his phallus in her every night and wake with it pressing for entrance into her pussy at each dawning. Never had she been so wet. It was as if her whole body was transmuting into honeyed fluid.

'Brad – Brad—' she moaned, as he continued to tongue her ear while his fingers at last penetrated between her secret lips.

He stroked the slick-wet aisle, measuring the quiver of excitement that flowed through her loins. His finger slid into her vagina, then when it was nicely wetted, smoothed it tenderly up her cleft and found that plump, hungry bud.

She sobbed out her pleasure, then fell silent, her eyes wide and vague, misted with that near orgasm trance. His mouth was on hers. He kissed her lips, then her breasts, nuzzling her nipples, biting and teasing the tips till she moved into him and clung with her arms about his neck, her face buried in his clean, sweet-smelling flesh.

It was not simply what he was doing, she had already experienced this before, it was more the way he worshipped wherever he touched, adoring her – loving her – wanting her and her alone. She was rising on warm, wet delirious waves of feeling, and, at the very moment of her climax, he held her off the bed, putting one hand between her buttocks, widening her crevice and sinking a finger into her convulsing aperture of bliss.

As the tension was released like a coiled spring and she shouted her ecstasy aloud, he held her close, kissing her mouth and nestling her damp sex in his hand.

'You came,' he whispered huskily. 'You came for me,' and he lifted the fingers that had known her secret place and pressed them to his nostrils, inhaling her fragrance.

'Now,' she muttered, gripping him fiercely, her legs locking round his waist. 'Put it in me. I want you – now!'

He knelt over her and she took his thick shaft between her hands and worked the enormous head up and down her slippery sex-lips. Brad grunted, suddenly rolled over on to his back, and drew her on top of him. He caught one of her breasts in his mouth as they hung above him, sucking the nipple hard, then he lifted her up so that her pussy was over his face. He ran his tongue round her entrance, licked her labia and nibbled at her clitoris.

'Oh, Brad,' she whispered unsteadily, bracing herself on the flat of her hands, eyes closed, head flung back, throat a long arch.

For answer, he kissed her bud, pulled it between his lips, tongued it hard. Heather came again, her body throbbing and pulsating, while he gave her clit a final mouthing and then moved her sharply down the length of his body till his thick, skyward-pointing cock sheathed itself in her vagina, wet with saliva and love-juice.

It was massive, filling her, driving home, and she jerked upright with the force of it, thighs spread wide, bearing down to take every inch, supporting her weight on a knee either side of him. She pumped hard, felt that extra hardening and twitching, felt him coming, spurting out a stream of hot nectar.

She fell forward across his chest, her buttocks in the air, his softening cock still buried within her folds. 'Blanche, my darling—' he murmured into her ear. 'I've wanted to do that for so long. Now I want to go on doing it for the rest of my life.'

So they did, or rather throughout the hours that remained of the night, trying all manner of ways in which to pleasure one another. At last Heather slept, nestled in his arms – a deep, contented slumber with her head resting on the matted fur of his chest, and her hand still holding his limp, wet and sticky penis.

'I always hold a party on Midsummer Eve,' Xanthia said. 'And tonight's the night. Friends come from all over. My parties are famous, or infamous, depending on your viewpoint. And it will be your last evening here, Heather, so make the most of it. I certainly intend to. I'm going to beat my own record of how many lovers I can have in a single night.'

At the appointed hour, Heather went out into the grounds. Near the lake stood a folly, fashioned as a Roman temple by one of Tostavyn Grange's former owners returning from his Grand Tour of Europe back in the 1700s.

It was early, but already the folly was filled, people moving about between the marble pillars or occupying the wide steps leading up to it, or seated on the grass beneath purple silk awnings that filtered the rays of the sunset and gave a subtle, flattering half-light. A warm breeze stirred the drapes, and roses, flaming scarlet and snowy white, filled the air with perfume that mingled with the heady scents used by both men and women.

A silvery cascade fountained into a marble basin where a bronze Neptune romped with a couple of bare-breasted mermaids. Venus, goddess of love, reigned supreme. Her representative was Xanthia, though that night she had chosen to be Valeria Messalina, Empress of the Roman Empire, known as the Illustrious Harlot.

Heather approached her where she lay on a couch beneath the awning. The long state banqueting tables were loaded with fruits, meats and wine, tapers glittering on gilded vessels. Divans were drawn up to them, piled with tapestry cushions. Xanthia's clients, also the actors and actresses, and a host of personal friends were gathered there, dressed as senators, poets, philosophers, grand ladies and notorious courtesans. The women were bejewelled, clad in pastel-coloured diaphanous robes, the men wearing togas and laurel wreaths.

195

Xanthia had never looked more beautiful. Her inky hair was drawn back showing her oval, sun-tanned face with its impish, pointed chin. Her full red lips were moist, her eyes outlined with kohl, the lids glistening with green-gold shadow. Above them her fine dark brows leaped upwards in a subtle curve. She wore a golden gown of sheer material through which her nipples peeped invitingly and, as she moved, it slid open, displaying her bare pubis with its deep, shadowy crease.

She held a hand out to Heather. Emerald bracelets winked and flashed. 'Come and sit by me, darling,' she crooned. 'How lovely you look. I knew an Ionic *chiton* would suit you. Such fragile linen, girded under your breasts. I can't keep my hands off you. I simply must play with them.'

Heedless of the crowd eating, talking and laughing on every side, Xanthia ran her fingers over Heather's breasts, then down across her stomach and pressed in between her legs. Heather's labia immediately dampened under that provocative touch, her bud itching to be stroked. The thin fabric added to the sensation, chafing the swelling clit, and Xanthia smiled into her eyes, rubbing it firmly. It was flattened by the taut pressure of the material but ready to burst nonetheless.

'I could make you come here and now,' she murmured. 'Shall I? Your first orgasm of the evening, or did you pleasure yourself while you were getting ready?

'No, I didn't,' Heather gulped, as Xanthia pulled her hand back and pleated the folds of the *chiton*. Though they were thick near her mound, Heather was aware of a wet patch impossible to disguise.

She could see Julie looking at it, her fingers

fondling her own nipples under an equally revealing gown. Her blonde curls were dressed high and fastened with a gem-studded fillet. She lolled on the divan next to André, who had one arm round her and the other across Xanthia's bare shoulders. He wore a short Greek-style tunic with a wide gold belt, and his large, semi-flaccid penis poked out from beneath it.

Julie's tongue licked over her lips at the sight. She extended a naked leg and her foot, encased in a sandal with criss-cross lacing, found its goal. She worked her big toe out of the straps and tickled André's prick. It immediately shot to full size.

By now, the guests were becoming lively, wine circulating freely, laughter raucous, voices rising excitedly. Xanthia stood up, clapped her hands, and at once a troupe of dancers whirled on to the grass. They were all perfect – six golden-skinned men and six equally beautiful girls.

The male dancers were athletic in build, and wore spiked leather collars, wide metal-studded armbands, and black hide straps that bound their bare chests. Their bellies were tightly contained by the shiny leather, thighs, too, and greaves covered their lower legs, ending in soft kid ankle boots. They were a cross between slaves and gladiators, and their costumes were open at the crotch, their testicles thrust forward, pricks arched, taut buttocks naked.

The graceful girls were attired as Bacchantes, each clad in a minute scrap of white chiffon, with a leopard skin over one shoulder. Breasts, nipples and mounds were exposed. Their hair, blonde, raven or red, tumbled around their faces from a circlet of vine leaves bound round their brows.

The band struck up, the music strangely compelling – flutes and drums, lyres and horns.

The dancers' movements were controlled and balletic, the passion of the girls and the strength of the men excitingly fierce and sensual – a vision of breasts, phalluses and alluring crevices.

The crowd roared approval, and now the dancers became inspired, twirling, leaping, the light translucent on bronzed limbs. Then the music died to a slow beat, and attention focused on one pair of performers. The girl twisted her body, sank to the floor. She was entirely naked, her breasts thrusting upwards, and her partner hovered over her, his arms opened wide like the wings of a bird of prey. She arched towards him, touching the ground with the back of her head and the tips of her toes, body forming a bridge. Her partner hovered above her, phallus erect, and she moved languidly till she could take it into her mouth.

Those watching craned forward in their seats. Some copied the antics on the grass, the flambeaux casting ruddy light over lovers already writhing and coupling. The principal dancers merged till their bodies seemed as one – the act of copulation raised to artistic heights, stunning to see. The corps de ballet also paired off, each couple winding their limbs around the other, cocks slipping into wet vaginas or penetrating the puckered, rosebud mouths of anuses.

But for Xanthia, the night had only just begun. 'And now, my friends – for my challenge,' she cried, silencing the clamour.

She dominated the gathering, this dark beauty, glittering in her golden gown with immense emeralds at her throat and on her arms. Her guests waited, slightly apprehensive. What was she planning to do now?

'Selina!' she called to a woman who reclined at the end of the table, a big-limbed, full breasted creature clad in Grecian robes.

'Empress?'

'You keep a brothel, don't you?'

'I do.' The woman smiled and entered into the game, having already been briefed.

'Who is your most famous whore?'

'Famous for beauty, for love – in which way famous?'

'Who has the record for the greatest number of lovers enjoyed in one night?'

There was laughter, and then argument between Selina and several of her girls. Xanthia watched and waited, imperious as the insatiable Roman Empress, her hand stealing to her breasts and caressing the satin skin.

'Well, don't you know?' she demanded impatiently. 'We will have a competition. There'll be prizes for the best performance. Are you game, Selina?'

'Done!' the actress replied.

'And who else?'

There was silence, then one or two voices spoke up, Julie's included. 'I will.'

'And will Rome not wager on her empress?' Xanthia asked of one of the senators. He hastily agreed.

'Then let the contest begin,' Xanthia cried, unfastening her gown, her body rising from its folds, blatant and beautiful.

Chapter Eleven

HEATHER WATCHED XANTHIA, Julie and several other women play the whore. Men were queueing to possess them, but she did not find it necessary to take up the challenge. In her book it was quality not quantity that counted. There would be a lover for her before the night was through, she was certain of it.

Even as she tried to relax on the couch, though the sights and sounds on every side were sexually stimulating, so she became aware of a form leaning over her and a voice murmuring,

'Good evening, milady.'

She glanced up into the eyes of the man who had played the gypsy, Jake. Her heart leaped. Her clitoris burned. All the heated memories of that afternoon in the dell shimmered in her brain and connected immediately with her loins.

'Hello yourself,' she replied. 'Didn't they have gypsies in Ancient Rome?'

He laughed, displaying even white teeth in that reckless, tanned face. 'I'm sure they did, but Xanthia decreed that I should be a soldier, a sort of Mark Anthony, if you like.'

'I do like,' she whispered, admiring his red kilt, the embossed breastplate, the wide belt supporting a short sword, the hair that had been cut to curl closely over his well-shaped head. 'You've slipped into the role perfectly.'

'I should do. I'm an actor by trade, but I'm not acting when I say that I couldn't forget you – Lady Heather.' He smiled down at her, and his hands came to rest on her shoulders. Big hands, strong and nimble. How well they had caressed the nooks and crannies of her most private places.

'We've no scenario to follow tonight,' she reminded him. 'Xanthia's dressed us up like this and provided the feast and entertainments, but it seems we're free to have whom we desire.'

His dark eyes smouldered in that exciting way she remembered so clearly. 'Shall we make up a scene of our own?' he suggested.

She went with him to a dark part of the garden and there lay down for him. There was no need for words. They came together sweetly and immediately. He wasn't Brad, but would do for the moment. Her lips parted as he kissed her, and a tingling sensation shot through her limbs, threatening to engulf her.

Oh, how convenient were these Greek gowns. So light, so flimsy, so easily pushed away. With her help, Jake unbuckled his armour, laying it aside. His cock came to rest in her hand of its own volition, unhampered by trousers. He was able to spread her open with ease, his fingers winding into her, stretching the walls of her vagina so that she oozed still more.

His penis was a fleshy spear, its head slick with moisture and she wanted to lick it off, to taste the salty juice. He rested on his back and she went down on him, greedy mouth enfolding his organ. It rose towards her, large and tense, and she controlled it utterly.

First she sucked it, then withdrew a little,

running her tongue up the hard trunk, while her hands gently massaged his balls. Round and round its tip she went, allowing him the delight of tiny teeth nips, but never too much. Opening her mouth wide, she took its length, deeper and deeper till it touched her throat.

Jake groaned his pleasure, gripping her head, keeping her still lest he yield and spill himself before time. 'Not yet,' he muttered. 'I don't want to come yet.'

She released him, and he raised her towards him till he could cover her lips with his. Her hot bud clamoured for him to rub it to orgasm, then have him entering her with his stiff and needy offering.

It happened as she desired. She was still trembling from her climax when he joined his flesh with hers, penetrating deeply, touching every tingling nerve-end. He was unable to hold back, his organ a power piston driving him to completion.

'I want to see you again,' he said when his breathing had slowed and they relaxed in each other's arms.

'You don't have to say that,' she protested gently. 'There's no commitment. We both know that we'll be fucking other people later tonight.'

His hand fondled her pussy, relishing the moist feel of it. 'I'm not saying we won't, but we've something special going between us. My career's beginning to take off. I'm flying to Australia next week to shoot a film. I've got the star part. Come with me and share my caravan on location in the outback.'

'I'll think about it,' she promised, lying there and enjoying his caresses.

'I know this is for real, Heather,' he insisted. 'Will you give me your phone number?'

She parted from Jake and wandered through the crowd. There was so much nudity and sex on every side that it became the norm – no longer shocking or particularly exciting. Xanthia was winning in the love Olympics, that much was obvious. Heather had never doubted that she would.

Music throbbed and people reached out to grab her as she passed, displaying their sex. One man dipped his penis into a glass of wine and then, laughing, held out the drink. She declined. A girl with boyish hips and coltish legs thrust forward her shaven pussy, offering it to Heather. Again, she smilingly refused and moved on. The dancers mingled with the crowd, making love to the senators and ladies.

Heather's head whirled, the noise, the plethora of bared genitals, the kaleidoscope of colours making her giddy. Seeking a moment's respite, she drifted away to Xanthia's private terrace.

There lay the pool, a restful blue, lit up by concealed lights below the surface. There was nothing Heather wanted more at that time than to sink into the placid water. She ungirded her *chiton*, took off her sandals and then walked down the wide tiled steps, first her ankles, then her calves and thighs immersed.

How glorious it was, cooled by the night air, but to blood-heat. Ah, yes, this was bliss! Her body was almost submerged, only the peaks of her breasts showing. She moved her legs, opening them slightly, feeling the gentle caress of the silky water on her inner parts. She thought about Jake and her groin felt heavy with desire, her clitoris stirring, alert and greedy, wanting satisfaction again.

Her fingertips found that bud of flesh in full erection as they sought and pressed it tenderly.

The other hand was busy, too, moving from nipple to nipple, applying friction to each in turn. Heather leaned her head back against the side of the pool, languidly pleasuring herself. She held back her climax. Even more than the final spasm, she had grown to love the surging sensitivity, the extreme tension, stroking the quivering stem, denying it the explosion for which it craved.

'Can I join you, or would you rather be alone?' a deep voice asked.

Heather opened her eyes, finger still pressing her pleasure point. She looked up to see Paul standing on the terrace. From his position above her he seemed incredibly tall, and extremely handsome, clad in the robes of an African tribesman.

'How come you're at a Roman feast?' she answered his question with one of her own, smiling, sleepy-eyed.

He grinned down at her, hands on his hips, magnificent in a colourful caftan decorated with *bartik* designs. It was trimmed with jaguar pelt. His locks were loose, ebony, ringletted, wild.

'The Romans sometimes put a captive on show, like a rare and exotic pet. He became their speciality, a novelty at their orgies. That's my role tonight.'

'You look wonderful,' Heather replied, swishing her legs in the water so that it lapped against her clit. She hoped that he would join her, remembering his glorious naked body, the gleaming, coffee-coloured skin, the rippling muscles, the large and impressive cock.

'Thank you, kind lady,' he grinned, admiring her with those melting brown eyes. 'I followed you here.'

'You did?' Joy stabbed through her but she tried to appear cool.

'I needed to be with you again.'

He started to undress, while she watched in shivering anticipation. He's like a god, she thought, so perfect an individual. He stepped down into the water and took her in his arms. Because she was shorter than him, his rising prick pressed against her waist, the naked glans sliding along her flesh.

He lifted her effortlessly, and she clasped her hands at the back of his neck beneath that cinnamon-scented hair, spreading her legs so that when he lowered her on to his cock he could penetrate her easily. He thrust upwards, his eyes slitting. Then he paused, his mouth level with her, kissing her, tongue delving deeply, all fragrance, warmth and wetness.

Feeling the hardness of the tiles at her back, she writhed as she clawed at his neck, sobbing and moaning, so frenzied that she was hardly aware that he was ejaculating. They threshed in the water, making waves, and when he withdrew, his face radiant, he still held her against him.

'We'll do it again in a while,' he promised. 'You didn't climax.'

'It doesn't matter,' she assured him, her hand beneath the water, holding his half-erect penis.

'Oh, but it does,' he answered solemnly. 'Long ago some of my ancestors were Zulus, and male honour couldn't be satisfied unless his partner came. A man who could bring a woman to orgasm was deemed a great warrior.'

They left the pool and, still wet and naked, made love again on a double lounger. He devoted himself to her, licking her sex, sucking her clit, rubbing it with the head of his penis until at last the pressure took command, lifting her to heavenly release. It was only then that he emptied himself into her vagina, his phallus

205

disgorging a milky torrent.

Resting on the lounger, they drank from the bottle of Calvados he had brought along. Heather felt so at ease with him, this beautiful creature who took pride in giving the greatest possible pleasure. He held her fingers in his own, and kissed them individually, nestled beside her in the afterglow, his cock lying along one brown inner thigh.

'I'm the singer in a funk band,' he said. 'I help Xanthia out for kicks and extra cash. We go back a long way, she and I. But I'm going on tour in Europe soon. I don't want to lose touch with you. Come with me.'

'As a groupie?' she replied with a giggle, thinking, my God, Mother would never live it down!

'No way!' he said quickly. 'You'll travel as my lady. The best hotels, the whole bit.'

'I'll let you know,' Heather said cautiously. She was unwilling to commit herself to anything at that moment.

'I'll give you my address and mobile phone number. I'm not often at home, spend most of my time at the recording studio. Can I have yours?'

He's indeed a beautiful fuck, she decided. A beautiful person, too. She couldn't make up her mind which she liked best, him or Jake, or even if it was necessary to make a choice. Presumably, it didn't matter.

'Enjoy 'em all!' Xanthia had advised. 'Play with their pricks, take your pleasure. Love 'em and leave 'em. You're free, girl. An independent lady. I hope you've learned that here.'

But it was Brad who wound up in her bed. Brad, gracious and distinguished in the robes of a Roman senator, who intercepted her in the small hours when she was dragging herself wearily upstairs, victim of too much excitement and too much brandy. She quickly discovered that though one might have too much of the latter, the former was inexhaustible.

'Are you an actor?' she asked as he slipped out of his robe in the shelter of her room.

'Nope,' he said, grinning across at her. 'I'm a businessman. I've known André for years. I've just gotten over a divorce and he suggested I give this place a whirl. I'm mighty glad I did, for I met you, Heather.'

'On the rebound?' she said quietly, hoping it wasn't so.

'Hell no! My wife was a bitch who took me to the cleaners. I'm well out of it.' He reached for her, adding, 'Come here, honey. I want to do wicked things to you.'

And he did, as the rising sun spread its flaming hues over the sky and the moon gave up the fight and retired. Heather was dizzied by him, his skill in rousing her surpassing all others. A sigh of pleasure shook her as she felt the exquisite need burning through her. Brad lifted her, carrying her across to the bed and, just for a moment, she was sure she could hear the strains of celestial music.

I'm crazy, she thought, while it was still possible to string coherent ideas together. I don't know him – well, only in the biblical sense. He, too, was terribly aroused. She could tell by his ragged breathing, but he took his time, paying special attention to erogenous zones other than her nipples and clit.

He kissed that sensitive spot where her neck joined her spine. Tongued the velvety rims of her ears. Ran his lips over her feet, sucking each individual toe, then up, up, across her knees, the insides of her thighs, and, at long last, permitted her to enjoy the feel of his tongue on her labia and swollen bud. Then, when she had climaxed several times, he slid his smooth, hard cock into the wet haven of her sex.

She clasped him tightly, pubis pressed to his so there wasn't a particle of space between them. She wanted him there for all time, filling every inch of her silken sheath, knowing each secret of her body. Visions drifted like delirium in her brain – Brad and her – travelling the world together – houses where they would live, decorated in mutual taste – children, miniature replicas of her and him. Sentimental notions of which Xanthia would heartily disapprove.

His prick entered her like a sword, the fire of it cleansing and healing her. she clasped her arms round his neck, and embraced him with her legs, longing to absorb every bit of him so that they became one united melding of flesh.

Dawn crept through the windows, casting rays across the polished boards, throwing bright patches on the ornate ceiling and the high four poster where Brad and Heather lay, oblivious to the world.

The candles and torches were guttering low. Sleeping figures lay about the grass or slumped on the folly's marble floor. Several had rolled from the divans, resting amidst the debris and wine-spillings. Xanthia raised herself from her couch, pushing away the naked black wrestler who still clung to her.

'Who wants to be next?' she cried exultantly. 'The contest has only just begun.!'

'You win. I've had enough!' moaned Julie, the only other competitor left in this sex marathon.

'Enough? You're a lightweight! I haven't warmed up yet.' Xanthia stretched her arms from which the jewels had been stripped and scanned her remaining guests. 'Give Samir a kick and wake him. He'll do.' She smoothed her hands over her breasts. They had been gilded, and there were still little flecks left to glitter almost inhumanly.

There were shouts and laughter, and Samir sleepily knuckled his eyes, ready to do his duty. After he had finished pumping her, and she had achieved her umpteenth orgasm, Xanthia gathered her long purple cloak about her naked body and stood on the temple steps, surveying the remnants of her party.

Her hair was damp and straggled across her make-up smeared face. The hand on the soft folds of the robe was limp, but there was the light of triumph in her eyes. Like her namesake, Messalina, who had loved to challenge the Roman harlots in a like manner, putting money on how many men she could take in a night, she had won her wager!

'I've come to say goodbye,' Heather said, as she strolled into Xanthia's private domain later that morning.

'Everyone's going,' Xanthia replied. 'I'll miss you particularly. Are you sure you want to leave? I was rather hoping you might help me run this place. We're always on the look out for talented, imaginative participants.'

'Thanks, but no thanks.' Heather shook her head firmly. 'I'm grateful for the way in which you've brought me out of myself, but now I'll take up my life from this point on.'

'I told you she wouldn't stay,' André commented, glancing at Xanthia fondly. 'Julie will. She's a natural, and I'm about to lose my secretary.'

He was wearing slacks and a tee-shirt, a light jacket slung over one shoulder, ready for the journey. He turned to Heather. 'We're off in half an hour. It'll be just you and me this time. Julie can't wait to help Xanthia get ready for the next batch of sex-hungry customers.'

'Thank you, but I shan't be driving back to town with you, André,' Heather said, perched on the balcony rail in the sunshine, one slim leg in loose tan palazzo pants swinging, the other braced on the tiled floor.

The paper-thin cheesecloth shirt she wore emphasised the generous swell of her breasts crowned by rosy nipples. *Sans* bra and panties, the lines of her body were uncluttered, and her hair flowed in a rich mane over her shoulders. She was free. Liberated. She planned to get rid of her chic suits. They no longer worked with her new persona. Her local charity shop would do well out of them, aid for Oxfam or somesuch.

'No?' His brows winged upwards. 'How so?'

'Someone else is taking me to London.' Heather could feel the blush rising to her sun-kissed cheeks.

'Ah ha! You're a dark horse,' Xanthia remarked, brazen as ever in a gauzy wrap, bare legs, bare feet, no underwear, her breasts bobbing and quivering as she moved. 'And who is it? Or aren't you telling? Let me think. Is it Jake or Paul or Brad? They're your favourite studs, aren't they?'

Heather shrugged, trying to appear nonchalant. 'If you must know, it's Brad.'

Xanthia shook her head in mock despair. 'What have I told you, Heather? Have you taken my advice seriously? You're falling for him. I can see it by the star in your eyes. Tut, tut!'

'Maybe I am, and there again, maybe I'm not,' Heather smiled. 'Don't worry about me, Xanthia. I've the phone numbers of the others and shall call them up if I feel like it.'

210

'Good girl. Play the field.' Xanthia roamed across to where André stood, elegant in his designer gear. She linked her arm with his and pressed her breasts into his chest. 'We wouldn't like you to get hurt, would we, André?'

'No, indeed. That wasn't the intention,' he answered, smiling into her shining eyes, his arm resting round her pliant waist.

Julie and Jason arrived then to say goodbye to Heather. 'I hope you'll be happy here,' she said, taking Julie's hands in her own, recalling their intimacy and the fun they'd shared.

'How could I not be? All that lovely cock free and gratis! It's paradise,' Julie laughed, running an appreciative hand over Jason's biceps, ready for sunning, swimming and fucking.

As Heather left the room with André, her last picture was that of Xanthia and Julie settled on the couch with Jason between them, while they pulled down his shorts and applied themselves earnestly to his genitals.

As Brad's Ferrari winged towards the Cornish-Devon border, she leaned her head against the leather, relaxed and happy, the warmth penetrating her core, rousing her to desire. Music poured from the speakers. He had slotted a disc into the CD which was an integral part of the dashboard, and a tenor voice rang out, singing Puccini's aria *Nessun Dorma*.

'Lovely,' she sighed. 'D'you like opera?'

'I'm crazy about it,' Brad answered, glancing at her from the tail of his eye. 'I've a box at the Met. We'll go there when we stay at my penthouse in New York.'

Was this man for real? she wondered, amazed. Could it be that she had found someone who would share her interests, as well as being the best screw she'd ever had?

It was thrilling to be so close to him in the intimacy of the interior, to see his hands in command of the wheel, lightly furred backs, long, strong fingers that had caressed her to a magnificent climax not many hours before.

She admired his hawklike profile, the proud curve of the nose, and firm, cleft chin. He had already asked her to go to America with him, actually owning a house in romantic New Orleans, but she hadn't yet given a definite answer. Lingering in her mind were memories of Paul and his chocolate-coated treat. Then there was Jake, so swarthy and smouldering. It would be fun to accompany him to Australia and watch him filming.

Three virile men, each a superb lover, each dying to feed on her mouth, suck her nipples, to lick and tongue her till her mind exploded in rainbow shards of sensation.

As Heather mused, so the itch began, her moisture dampening the seam of her pants, the friction of her nipples against the cheesecloth almost painful. Then, on a fresh uprush of lust, she remembered her other option.

Xanthia had opened her senses, heart and mind to the love of women. Endlessly sensual, all softness, sweetness and precious delight. The icing on the cake. And, in between whiles, there was always a vibrator.

Was ever a girl so spoilt for choice?

The disc finished, and Brad's free hand came to rest on her knee, slid upwards, opened her legs a little and brushed her bud through the cotton pants. All the while he never took his eyes from the road, caressing her casually, his middle finger pressing the material against her furrow.

Heather squeezed her thighs together at the exquisite feeling, then he lifted his hand, untied the drawstring of her pants and dived inside. He walked his fingers across her tanned belly to where the feathery hair formed a triangle. He touched her palpitating button, hard and wet for their mutual entertainment, and her heart beat wildly as the pleasure gushed through her. She reached the summit, her orgasm one of fearful intensity.

She leaned dizzily against Brad's shoulder, and he didn't withdraw his hand at once, cradling her mound. They were driving through a wooded area, quiet and secluded under the noonday heat. He rolled the car off the road, braked, got out and went round to open the passenger door. He drew her up to him, treating her to his quirky smile.

'Honey, I'm going to lay you,' he announced.

'Here?' She tried to wriggle free, a trace of conservatism breaking through the trance. 'Someone might see us.'

For answer, he tightened his arm round her waist and guided her down a bank. Immediately they were screened from the road by thick trees and undergrowth. Brad pressed her against the knobbly bark of an ancient oak, its dense foliage forming a canopy over their heads. The blood pounded through her groin at his urgency. No smile on his face now, just the intense, lusting look of a man who needs to bury his shaft in his woman's body without delay.

His mouth sank on hers as if to assuage a raging thirst, and his hands roughly thrust aside the deep opening of her shirt, finding the jutting nipples, rolling them, teasing them. She clung to him with savage desperation, knowing that she could lose herself in this man so very easily, sacrificing her hard-won independence to a kind of enchanted slavery – his for ever, her mind, her body, maybe even her soul.

She needed him, ached for his possession, dissolving in the molten heat of his desire. Her lips opened under his, the tip of her fiery tongue darting out. She had longed for him to kiss her since the moment she had seen him leaning indolently on his car outside the Grange, waiting for her. His mouth was wonderful, moving over hers with savage insistency, a part of her existence now.

Then, somehow, her trousers fell down about her ankles. Her loose shirt was wide open and he was unzipping his own trousers, drawing her inside and against his warm body, his erect cock nudging into her, seeking its destination. The bark scraped along her spine as he raised her, supporting her weight while she parted her legs. With a grunt, he impaled her on that iron-hard penis.

Her breath escaped in a great rush at this almost brutal invasion. Mouth pressed to open mouth they hung there for a second, then, hands cupping her buttocks, he slid her up and down the length of his shaft, grunting with exertion every time it reached the point of deepest penetration.

The leafy canopy, the sun-flecked bower whirled giddily as mad pleasure crackled through Heather's veins. She moaned his name over and over. She wanted to be used by him, to give herself utterly. Her hands stroked his chestnut hair and pummelled the broad, muscular shoulders as she rode him to completion, feeling the force gathering in his loins ready to explode in a fierce, lava-like stream.

He was wracked by a final convulsion, heaving against her, then slumping with his face buried in her hair, penis slipping out of her wet pussy. He gently and carefully lowered her till her feet met solid earth. When she was safely grounded he released her, zipping up his fly.

Heather leaned against the tree, eyes closed, unwilling to return to reality. His warmth was gone and she felt bereft.

Then he spoke. 'I'm sorry, darling. I should've satisfied you, too. We'll do it again soon and you won't be disappointed, I promise.'

She looked at him, smiling, limp, blissfully content. 'I came in the car. Remember?' she murmured. 'It was your turn.'

He threw back his head and laughed, then stretched out a hand and clasped hers. 'We've plenty of time to try it every which way. Do you have to go right home? Couldn't we book into some quaint little pub somewhere, order room service, and stay there for days? I want to fuck the ass off you.'

'Why not?' she replied, linking her fingers with his as they strolled back to where the Ferrari gleamed under the summer sun.

I can do what I like, she realised with sudden conviction. I shan't go back to Mother. When I'm in London I'll stay in my apartment. Now, all that matters is making this relationship work.

I hope it does, but if, and God forbid, it fails, then it may break my heart for a while, but I know it won't be the end of the world. I have plenty of alternatives.

In the car again, the engine revving, she turned to Brad, hugging his arm and saying, 'Put on that

CD again. I'll always associate it with this moment – the woods, the sky – and making love with you.'

Teaching the Temptress
Ginnie Bond

' "Oh my God," she whispered as tears came into her
eyes, and her whole body began to quiver. Then he rose
and placed a line of little licks up her stomach to her
breasts. Each nipple was taken in its turn and teased
tenderly with in-turned lips . . .'

Ferne Daville is twenty-five, extremely wealthy,
and runs the family conglomerate with an iron
hand. Schooled to this from birth, she lives for the
business at the expense of her happiness, her feelings held in tight check.

But after a highly charged encounter at a masked
ball she had no wish to attend, Ferne finds herself
propelled from one erotic experience to the next, as
if by design; as if someone is deliberately intent on
melting her icy façade; as if someone is determined
to teach Ferne how to become a temptress . . .

Legacy of Desire

Marina Anderson

'*Davina started to tremble. The camisole top was sheer; Jay would be able to see everything through it, including her shamefully hard nipples. She wished that he'd touch her. Her breasts were aching for the feel of his hands on them while her body had become unbelievably sensitive . . .*'

Davina Fletcher has a comfortable life and a comfortable boyfriend until the death of her uncle changes all that. As her home and artist's studio are in the grounds of his house, she always assumed that she would inherit everything. Instead she finds she has a new landlord in the shape of tall, dark and handsome Jay Prescott, an American lawyer with a taste for Davina's paintings – and soon for Davina herself.

If she is to continue living at the house, she must be obliging towards Jay and his friends but soon she realises he has an unconventional way of collecting the rent. In order to keep her home, she must be a player in his games but the power he wields is far stronger than just that of landlord . . .

Other X Libris fiction, available by mail or from
www.xratedbooks.co.uk

X LIBRIS BOOKS
Cash Sales Department, P.O. Box 11, Falmouth, Cornwall, TR10 9EN
Tel: +44 (0) 1326 569777, Fax: + (0) 1326 569555
Email: books@barni.avel.co.uk.

POST AND PACKING:
Payments can be made as follows: cheque, postal order (payable to X Libris Books) or by credit cards. Do not send cash or currency.

U.K. Orders under £10	**£1.50**
U.K. Orders over £10	**FREE OF CHARGE**
E.E.C. & Overseas	**25% of order value**

Name (Block Letters) _____

Address _____

_____

Post/zip code: _____

☐ Please keep me in touch with future X Libris publications

☐ I enclose my remittance £ _____

☐ I wish to pay by Visas/Access/Mastercard/Eurocard

Card Expiry Date

☐☐☐☐☐☐☐☐☐☐☐☐☐☐☐☐ _____